COME SEPTEMBER

By
Virginia Bickel

PublishAmerica
Baltimore

© 2006 by Virginia Bickel.
All rights reserved. No part of this book may be reproduced, stored in a retrieval system or transmitted in any form or by any means without the prior written permission of the publishers, except by a reviewer who may quote brief passages in a review to be printed in a newspaper, magazine or journal.

First printing

This book is a work of fiction. Names, characters, places, and incidents are products of the author's imagination or are used fictitiously. Any resemblance to actual events or locales or persons, living or dead, is entirely coincidental.

ISBN: 1-4241-1500-0
PUBLISHED BY PUBLISHAMERICA, LLLP
www.publishamerica.com
Baltimore

Printed in the United States of America

Dedication

To the memory of my late husband, John W. Bickel; my first-born, Illa Bickel Conklin; my first-born son, John W. Bickel; my youngest, Perry E. Bickel; and their wonderful families.

Chapter 1

Nonie Lee wrote:

March 30
Dear Diary,
    My father's voice trembled as he spoke, "Ed, I read in the morning paper that that Tillie woman died last night."
    Mr. Thompson said, "Really? That comes as a shock; what happened?"
    "The word they are putting out is that she died of a heart attack. However, I hear from a reliable source that her plump body was found lying face-down in a deep-burgundy pool of her own blood, in a dank and dark jail cell, remote from the other prisoners. All the while the Congressional staffers worked tirelessly through the night preparing their bosses for today's sworn tell-all. Most convenient for the powers that be and the special interest types."
    "Reliable source, you say?"
    "Yes, don't forget I'm in the newspaper business. We'll have to think of someway to keep my daughter safe; we know now that those SOBs will stop at nothing, even murder."
    "Now listen, Fred, as your attorney and your friend I'm advising you not to panic; it's time for calm, cool-headed thinking; it'll work out. Come on down to my office and we'll figure out something."
    Dad came home late from his meeting with Mr. Thompson that night. He called Mother and me. "You ladies come on downstairs. I come bringing good news and steamers from Starbucks. I even picked up a square of gingerbread while I was in there." He tried to sound nonchalant, even jolly. We were up most of the night hearing Dad and Mr. Thompson's plan for me.

March 31
Dear Diary,
Tomorrow I'll no longer be me. It has been arranged for me to cease to exist as Nonie Lee Talbert, at least for some time to come. April 1, I'll be assigned a new name and a new home. Aw, April Fool's Day, what a coincidence! I hope I can fool all those people who have been threatening me. When I disappear from the Washington scene the word will be passed around newsrooms that I am backpacking in Europe, aiming for a trip around the world before returning home. Only my agent, Hal Hollis, Ed Thompson, my mother and father and Rob will know this is not true. I'll miss my family and friends, but my very life may be at stake. I'll spend the rest of today readying for my disappearance: changing type of clothes, my hairstyle and color; glasses will be added, nice big black horned-rimmed ones should do the trick.

One year later a young woman gazed at the crest of Mt. Franklin in the distance and tried to picture Benjamin Franklin's profile. The story goes, she thought, that they named the mountain after the illustrious Mr. Franklin because of the likeness to his profile silhouetted there in the jagged rock against the cloudless sky. *Darned if I see any resemblance to ol' Ben's profile up there among the rocks.* Averting her attention away from the mountain she realized she was in front of the store she was looking for. Looking in the window at the new books on display, she picked up her pace and headed for the door. She felt a jolt in the back of her head and heard something that sounded like a coconut being hit with a hammer. Suddenly, she found herself lying face down on the sidewalk. She lay there on the hot concrete, too stunned to move.

She felt someone turn her over on her back and place sturdy hands under her arms to lift her to her feet. Her knees buckled. As she crumpled to the ground, the person behind her went down with her, cradling her head in his lap. She heard a voice that sounded far away. "Don't move. It's best you stay where you are for a minute." Thousands of tiny lights swirled around in her senses as she tried without success to see where the voice was coming from. She heard someone moan, "Oooh, ooh." She didn't realize the moans were her own. She mumbled; she thought she was saying, "It hurts, please, not again."

Then as if coming from deep within a well, she heard voices; someone was giving a command, "Dammit, Larry, hurry. I think we'd better take her inside and get a cold cloth on her head. She's had a nasty fall. Cynthia, call an ambulance."

"Dan, you aren't supposed to move an injured person before an ambulance arrives," a female voice answered.

"We'll worry about that later."

Someone was slapping the inside of her wrist. "Wake up, wake up." She wanted to tell them she would be all right in a minute. She tried and thought she said no ambulance, but her lips didn't move. She felt herself being placed on a hard surface. Gentle hands placed a cold compress on her forehead. Someone was slapping the inside of her wrist, "Wake up, wake up." She couldn't respond; darkness enveloped her. She heard no more.

Daniel Lindsey took a handkerchief from his back pocket and wiped the sweat from his brow. "Damn, it's hot out here. We can't leave her out here on this sidewalk. We have to get her inside, now."

"Look at this." Cynthia lifted a silver pendant hanging on a silver chain around the woman's neck and said, "Trudy." Then turning the pendant over, "Here on the other side a rose is engraved. Her name must be Trudy."

Daniel asked, "Do you think her name could be Trudy Rose?"

"It's possible," Cynthia answered. "And I think probable."

The ambulance came and took her away. Daniel asked Larry to look after the store for a while. He and Cynthia followed the ambulance to the hospital hoping to find out the prognosis. They were asked many questions by the admitting clerk at the hospital, "Who is this woman? What do you think she was doing on Mesa Street? Why is her face scratched and bruised?"

To all the questions, Daniel answered, "We don't know; we found her on the street in front of my store, The Bookmark."

The following morning, soon after opening the store, Cynthia and Daniel were having coffee when Larry stopped by to bring the morning paper. Handing it to Cynthia he said, "Thought you would like to see what the *El Paso Times* has to say about what happened in front of The Bookmark yesterday."

Opening the paper, Cynthia said, "Here it is. 'According to Mr. Daniel Lindsey, owner of The Bookmark Book Store, yesterday around noon a woman was found unconscious in front of his store on Mesa Street. The bruises and scratches on her face indicate that she fell face down on the pavement. The only identification found on her was a small silver pendant on a chain around her neck with the word "Trudy" engraved on one side and on the other side the likeness of a rose. The police are hoping that someone will come forward to identify her. Officer Thad Jones said there has been no report of a missing person in the area. An investigation is underway.'"

"After hearing Cynthia read the account of what happened Daniel said, "If I had kept after the city to fix that damn crack, this would not have happened."

"Will you come off it, Dan," his brother Larry said. "I've told you before, it's not your fault she fell. You know you have called the city several times about that crack."

Daniel said, "Nevertheless, since the incident happened in front of the store, I think we have an obligation to keep an eye on her progress, do anything we can to see that she gets what she needs until the police can find out who she is and notify her folks."

For a time thereafter, time was lost to the girl wearing the silver necklace. Doctors, nurses and all others knew her only as Trudy Rose.

Folding the paper and placing it on the counter, Daniel said, "A week since Trudy's accident and still no one has come forward to inquire about her. I'm glad they aren't calling her Jane Doe, like they usually call an unknown female person. Cynthia, if you can stay with the store for a while, I'll run over to the hospital and see how things are coming along."

Cynthia nodded. "Be off then, but try to be back by noon."

Daniel arrived at the hospital in time to catch Dr. Tilford at the nurses' station just as he was finishing up Trudy's chart. "How's it going, Doctor?"

"We're lucky in one respect; no bleeding showed up on the CAT scan. Most likely the fall caused general swelling, which led to a coma. Until the swelling goes down she will remain unconscious. We have to hope the swelling does not worsen and prevent blood flow to her brain."

Dr. Tilford said, "The thing that puzzles me is how she got an injury on the back of her head and on her face. Only thing I can figure is that she fell on her back and in shock turned, squirming, on her stomach."

Daniel nodded. "That does seem odd. Is it alright for me to go in to see her?"

"I'd rather you didn't. They are busy in there, getting her on a ventilator."

Alarmed, Daniel asked, "Ventilator?"

"Cool it, Dan; the ventilator is just to help with the swelling; it would be better if you wait a day or two to see her."

With an air of resignation, he said, "Thank you, Doctor. Please let me know of any changes."

"Will do. Take care."

Daniel walked away, disappointed that he couldn't see her, but he knew the doctor was right. The next two days passed slowly, but after that with the aid of his mother, sister, and brother helping out in the store, Daniel managed to be at her bedside for at least an hour, more if he could spare the time, hoping to be there when she awakened. He didn't want her to wake up alone and not know where she was or how she got there. He chided himself over and over for the next few days; nothing his folks said diminished his feeling of guilt that she fell in front of his store.

In the hospital room he watched her even, silent breathing and wondered who she was and where she came from. Still, no one had been reported missing in the near vicinity of El Paso, or anywhere else in Texas. He remembered that when she was admitted to the hospital, she wore a lone platinum ring—a sapphire set between two small diamonds. On her wrist she wore a large silver watch on a white leather band and small silver earrings graced her pierced ears. He watched her day after day, her jet-black hair flowing out over the white pillow slip. Her pale face, scratched and swollen from the fall, closed eyes, and unmoving lips, showed no sign of consciousness. As time passed, he began to wonder if the ring was an engagement ring; he wasn't sure why, but he hoped it was not.

After a week, Daniel made a point of being in Trudy's room when Dr. Tilford was present. "What can we do to get her awake, Doctor? Don't you think we need to call in a specialist?"

"I'm way ahead of you there, Dan; I had a neurologist look at her yesterday. His finding was the same as mine. He thinks her brain is swollen from the hard blow she took to the head when she hit the hard concrete. About all that can be done now is to give her medication to reduce the swelling; that's one of the medicines in the drip you see flowing into her vein."

"Shouldn't she be reacting to something by now?"

"Patience, fellow, it will take time for the swelling to go down."

"I've been talking to her like you recommended. Only thing, not knowing her, it's hard to think of something to talk to her about. I just keep asking her questions, some of them over and over, things like her name, where she lives, such as that. The bruises on her face and forehead are starting to fade some, becoming a lighter purple. Isn't that a good sign?"

"Yes, I suppose it is, but what we have to worry about is her bruised brain. I'm sure that is why she is not responding to stimuli. We have pricked her finger with a pin, no indication that she feels anything. Until the swelling goes down, her brain will not be getting the flow of blood it needs; that explains her comatose condition."

Back in the nation's capital, a mother and father were worried; there had been no word from Ed Thompson in two weeks. "Do you think he hasn't had word from her agent since she left Seattle?" the mother fretted.

"Oh, I think her agent is just waiting until she gets back to the island; then he will report after he hears how her promotion trip turned out. You know she planned to visit several cities before returning to the island. He'll let us know when he hears from her. We'll get a call any day now telling us all is well." Her father tried to reassure her mother, and tried to believe what he was saying.

"Maybe, but I think you should call him; I want to know what is going on. I think her leaving the island was a mistake. I'm concerned for the life of our daughter. Maybe she shouldn't have gone into hiding. Maybe that woman she was interviewing died of natural causes, maybe there was no cause for alarm and that all this hiding was brought on by our being overly anxious."

"You could be right, dear, but I didn't want to take chances with our daughter's life. Let's wait until Rob gets back; he'll know what to do. He'll be back in town soon."

A few days after Daniel's talk with Dr. Tilford, he walked into room 447 to find Dr. Tilford bending over Trudy's bed; he was lifting her eyelids, shining a pin light in her eyes. Daniel rushed to his side, "How is she doing, Doctor? Do you think she'll wake up and if she does, do you think she'll have amnesia?"

"We won't know that for sure until she is fully awake and alert. I can't be certain but I do think she will wake up. At first we thought the coma could be caused by a concussion as well as bruising of the brain, but that is not the case; no concussion showed up on the x-ray. It's most likely caused by the cranial swelling as we have thought all along." He could see that the young man was becoming more weary and haggard every day. Trying to put a good face on the situation to allay Daniel's fear he repeated, "As I said, there is some cranial swelling. That is most likely the reason she is comatose, unless it is an emotional trauma caused by the shock of the sudden fall. After all, sustaining a fall like that must be quite traumatic. We have found no reason for the coma other than the swelling."

"Do you think she'll pull out of it?"

"To answer your question again, Dan, about whether she will live, which I think is what you are really asking, yes I think so. However, when the brain swells, it is held captive, so to speak, by the skull; that prevents expansion and pressure results. Less oxygen slows the healing process. We'll just have to wait and see how her body reacts to the treatment. We have to give it time to work. Try not to worry; her vital signs are good. As I told you before, one of those bags is dripping a medication into her veins that also helps to reduce the swelling and heal the injured tissues so blood can carry oxygen to the brain."

"What is your best guess as to when she'll come out of this? When she will awaken?"

Dr. Tilford was becoming weary of Daniel's constant questions. "It could be today, tomorrow, next week or never. At this point we have no way of knowing."

"So we just have to play a lousy wait and see game?"

"That's about it." Dr. Tilford put his arm around Daniel's shoulders. "Now run along and tend to your store. No amount of fretting will help. It will only wear you down so you will not be able to do anything for her when and if she does regain consciousness; and I think she will. I'm now expecting a favorable outcome."

"Thanks, Dr. Tilford. It makes me feel better to hear you say that."

After two weeks of worry, Daniel was happy to see that the bruises on Trudy's face were clear and the swelling gone. His joy was heightened when he saw her eyelids flutter, then open just a bit. He could see just a part of her quivering eyeballs peeking from under dry eyelids. He waited impatiently hoping her eyelids would finally open all the way. As he waited, Nurse Abigail came striding into the room; her stiffly starched blue cotton pants suit made a swooshing sound as she walked.

Daniel turned to her. "She opened her eyes just for a moment. I think that means she is waking up, don't you?"

"Mr. Lindsey, try to relax. You know Dr. Tilford feels confident that she will awaken once the swelling in her brain has gone down. Let's see if I can get some reaction from her." She used her most commanding voice. "Trudy, Trudy, listen to me. Squeeze my hand if you hear me. Great, great; a small pressing on my fingers; now talk to me. What is your name?"

Opening her eyes briefly, the young woman groaned and stirred restlessly.

Daniel asked, "The swelling in her face has gone down. Isn't that an indication that the brain should be reacting the same way?"

"It would seem so. Now please go, I have to take her vitals."

Daniel was pleased two days later when he walked into her room and saw that the ventilator had been removed. He barely got seated beside her bed when she began to stir. She opened her eyes; she looked surprised, then frightened when she saw the blurred image of a man sitting in a chair beside her bed. She winced as she spoke; her throat was parched, "What happened? Where am I?" she asked in a weak, husky voice. "Who are you?"

Thank God I'm here. "I'm Daniel Lindsey. You took a nasty fall, bumped your head on a cement sidewalk and passed out. We called an ambulance and..."

"No, no ambulance. I'll be fine in a minute. Please, no ambulance, hear me, no ambulance."

Daniel chuckled. *Oh Lord, she doesn't know she has been in a coma, she thinks it just happened.* "You tripped on a crack in the pavement and went down. You have been in this hospital room for two weeks. By the time you could speak it was a little late to request no ambulance."

Her eyes were darting this way and that. "Oh no, no," she croaked. "No ambulance." she repeated, "no one must know...." She seemed to check her words in mid-sentence as if a sudden thought came to her, warning caution. "No one must know."

No one must know? Know what? Daniel wondered. "Is there someone we can call? Parents? A husband? A friend?"

"No, no one, I don't think," she stammered. "Someone to call? Is there someone? Maybe...." She closed her eyes and drifted off for a minute.

"Wait, wait, don't go to sleep. Talk to me. Tell me your name. Come on, Trudy. Stay with me here. Tell me your name; we need to notify your folks that you are here."

Her eyes started moving more slowly. She opened them wide and haltingly asked, "You say I fell? No, someone hit me. Where am I? Hospital room? I said no ambulance."

Daniel could see that she did not understand the conversation they had earlier. *She's like a phonograph record; she's stuck in that 'no ambulance' groove. I wonder what she is afraid of?* "As I said, you tripped over a crack in the pavement in front of my store; you took a nasty fall."

She whispered through still slightly swollen lips, her voice hoarse and barely audible. "I remember, something hit the back of my head and someone grabbed my briefcase. Where is my bag?"

That accounts for the injury to the back of her head as well as the bruises and scratches on her face. "Your bag? Did you have a handbag?"

"I think I did." She hesitated. "Yes, I did," she mumbled.

Now Daniel realized something was terribly wrong. The mugger must have wanted something she carried in her briefcase. " What was in your briefcase?"

"I had...oh, something important."

"Something important? What?"

"I, I'm not sure, but, but important."

"Can you tell me your name?"

"Of course, I'm…I'm….Who are you?"

"My name is Dan, remember? I told you. You say you think someone mugged you? I didn't actually see you fall, but I thought you stumbled on a crack in the sidewalk."

She spoke through parched lips; her words were slow and slurred. "My briefcase. I had, oh I, I'm tired. Did you say two weeks? Have I been asleep that long?"

"You've been in a coma. Please, try to remember your name and I'll notify your parents, or maybe a husband?"

"My name? My name is…" She looked frightened. "Where is my bag?"

"We found no handbag." Her heavy, even breathing told Daniel that she had drifted into a deep sleep again. It also told him she was not yet well enough to answer questions. He hoped she didn't slip back into a coma.

He pushed the call button. "Nurse, nurse, come quick."

Nurse Abigail walked hurriedly into the room, a concerned look on her face. Her short cropped red hair and dark snappish eyes gave the impression that she would brook no foolishness. She barked, "What happened?"

"Nothing bad," Daniel assured her. "Trudy opened her eyes for a couple of minutes and said a few words. I'm wondering what it means."

"It means she is still alive," Nurse Abigail said tersely. Her impatience was evident as she flounced around to the other side of the bed. "Too bad you didn't keep her awake. If that happens again call us immediately. Keep her awake until we get in here."

"I tried, but there was no way. She just stopped talking, closed her eyes and was gone, back into a deep sleep. I tried to awaken her again, I wanted to find out her name, but..."

"Next time, don't fool around trying to talk to her. Call me immediately."

"Yes ma'am." He felt he should snap his heels and salute.

"When will the doctor be in? I want to talk to—"

Nurse Abigail interrupted. "The doctor will be in around seven this evening. Today is Thursday. the doctor's afternoon to relax, play golf, whatever." Implicit in her tone was "and don't bother him."

Chapter 2

Daniel looked at his watch. *Too darn long to wait*, he thought. As soon as she left the room he picked up the phone and dialed nine for an outside line.

"Dr. Tilford's office," came a cheerful answer.

"Hello, this is Dan Lindsey; I'm calling about Trudy Rose. May I speak to the doctor, please?"

" I'll see if the doctor is available." Click, she was gone.

Daniel stood on one foot then the other, rubbing the back of his neck with his free hand, waiting for what seemed several minutes. His neck felt stiff, and he was beginning to get a headache. Finally he heard, "Hello, Dan, how's it going there?"

"Doctor, I'm glad I caught you, thought you'd be on the golf course."

"Had to come in, had an emergency. So what's up?'

" I think it's good news; at least I hope it is. I'll have to let you decide. Trudy woke up for a couple of minutes today and said a few words. When I asked her name she said she was tired; I couldn't keep her awake."

"That is good news. Wakefulness is a good sign. For only a couple of minutes, you say?"

"Yes, that's what worries me. I tried to keep her awake because I wanted to find out her name. I don't know any more than I did before except that she says she was hit on the back of her head, and that the mugger took her briefcase and her handbag is missing. Frankly, I think she is afraid of something or someone."

"Really? Why do you think that?"

"She looked scared when I questioned her about her name. Furthermore, she said, 'No one must know.'"

"Know what?"

"I don't know. That's what I asked her. I wanted her to talk to me, maybe tell me what she meant, but that's when she went back to sleep."

"If you can wait there, I'll come in as soon as I finish with this patient. We'll talk then."

"I'll be here, but listen, Doctor, don't call the police about her saying she was mugged. She is in no shape for questioning yet; she is probably unreliable at this point."

Forty-five minutes later Dr. Tilford walked into room 447. He was a man of medium build, a neat but informal dresser. His chestnut hair was beginning to show streaks of gray. He sported a well-trimmed, almost red mustache, which gave him a natty appearance. He found Daniel slumped in a chair beside Trudy's bed. Daniel wore his usual khaki slacks and blue oxford cloth shirt, no tie, but he wasn't his usual neat self. His blue eyes looked tired, and his dark blond hair was rumpled and in need of a barber's attention. He hadn't taken time for a haircut since the morning Trudy was hurt.

Dr. Tilford took his pinlight from his pocket, lifted Trudy's eyelids and shined the light into her eyes. "Constricted pupils, good sign." He took her pulse and blood pressure. After he called her name several times, he noted a slight movement of her upper lip. She groaned and muttered something unintelligible.

Doctor Tilford looked up at Daniel. "You mentioned a briefcase. Was she carrying anything important?"

"She wasn't clear about that. I don't know if she couldn't remember or if she was deliberately vague. After she said, 'No one must know,' she didn't finish the sentence. It was as if she thought about something that frightened her. That's why I think she is afraid of something. By the way, she said she was hit on the back of the head; was there any indication that that happened? I didn't see any blood in her hair or notice a lump."

"That's understandable; it probably had not started swelling before the ambulance came for her. Besides it was a small lump and she has been on her back most of the time since, no way you would notice it. Anyway, I think it was the fall on her face that caused most of the damage. Remember her forehead had a large gash that required fourteen stitches to close."

"Then she was mugged, as she insists. Somebody must have wanted what she had in her briefcase, but why would they take her handbag, or if they wanted her bag, why did they take her briefcase? If it was just a simple robbery why didn't they take her jewelry?"

"Those are questions for the police. Perhaps when she fell the culprit panicked and didn't wait to finish the job; take her jewelry I mean. It's possible the mugger took her bag to make it look like a simple robbery. That business about her saying no one must know does worry me. We'll have to tell the police she thinks she was mugged. They've been going on the assumption that she stumbled and fell."

"Not yet, Doctor; as I said, she is not coherent enough for questioning now. It might get her upset, slow her progress."

"We'll see."

"What's the prognosis, Doctor?"

He smiled as he turned to Daniel. "To answer your question, I'd say her prognosis is a good bit better now than it was yesterday or the day before. We'll have to wait for the diagnosis before we are sure."

"The diagnosis? I don't think she has amnesia. She remembers she was mugged."

"Dan, I think I told you before, we'll have to wait until she is fully awake. She may have slipped back into a coma, maybe now she is just in a drug-induced sleep, or maybe she is just tired like she said."

"How could she be tired? She's been asleep for three weeks. She must have that kind of amnesia where she can remember some things and not others, otherwise she would have been able to tell me her name and give other details: where she lives, some person to call, what she was doing on Mesa Street that morning."

We don't know what kind of demons she's fighting while she sleeps. An injury to the brain can have strange effects. It won't help to get all shook up and start imagining things are worse than they are. Let's just relax and let time, the great healer, along with the medication, take its course."

He didn't like the worried look on Daniel's face. He was concerned that he might be getting too involved with the care of this girl, a girl about whom nothing is known. "Dan, if it is true that she was hit on the head by some unknown person, for some unknown reason, we can rest easy that the crack in the sidewalk had nothing to do with her fall. Quit beating yourself up about it. It's time to let the police take charge. You need to get more rest and take care of your business."

"My business is doing fine. My sister Cynthia is my assistant. Since this happened, my brother Larry has been helping out when he can spare the time. My mother loves helping out in the store, and she has spent time here with Trudy as well. So you see, I've had a lot of help."

"Nevertheless, it's time for the police to know what is going on with her; know that she thinks she was hit on the head and something, probably something of value, taken from her. Perhaps there was something in that briefcase that could shed some light on what this is all about. You know, Dan, there could be criminal activity going on here."

"Doctor, I'm asking you as a favor to me, will you please wait until she has recovered her memory before notifying the police about the mugging? There is nothing they can learn from her until she is alert."

"Dan, you are asking me to do something that I don't want to do; I don't think it is right. Besides, she may not ever recover her memory. The less time lapses before the police start an investigation, the more likely they are to find out the nature of the crime. They need to be looking for a possible link to a crime, maybe even organized crime, and not just an accident or a simple mugging."

"But, Doctor, please give her a little more time. We don't know for sure that she was mugged. In her present state we can't put too much stock in her ramblings."

"All right, Dan, just a short time more, then we must let the police take over. In the meantime I want you to remember that we know nothing about this girl. She may be married, have sixteen kids and a dog that bites," Dr. Tilford chuckled. *Or worse,* he thought, *she may be a criminal, maybe wanted by the FBI.*

"I know. I've thought about all that, except the part about the dog," Daniel smiled. "I know what you are getting at, but I can handle it, whatever it is."

"Well, just think about it before you go off the deep end. I've known your family for a long time, Dan, known you for a long time, and I don't want to see you get hurt. If your father, God rest his soul, were here he would give you the same advice. There'll be time enough to sort things out when we find out more about what happened that day and why." He paused, placed his hand on Daniel's shoulder and continued. "Listen to me, Dan, I can see you are getting far too emotionally involved with this girl. This may take a while to clear up. Many times, memory loss is restricted to experiences closely related to the accident. Other times the patient may have complete recall of things that happened before, but no memory of what happened immediately after the incident. There is another possibility. She may not remember anything about her life before the accident. That is the worst scenario other than her not recovering at all. If this woman has amnesia, it could be caused by emotional shock as well as actual injury to the brain. We don't know if the swelling in her brain is enough to cause such a deep and sustained coma. There is nothing on the scan to indicate a laceration of any sort to the brain. When amnesia is caused by injury, it may cause changes in the brain, making recall impossible, but since no brain injury showed up on her scan, other than a slight bruising which is causing the swelling, it may be caused by an emotional problem. That may very well be the case, brought on by the shock of the blow to the head; hypnosis or drugs may treat it. We may very well resort to one or the other of these methods if the amnesia persists too long. We just have to have patience; as we discussed, it's a wait and see game."

"I understand."

"Do you now?" *I doubt it.* "Go home and get some needed rest."

"I know it is a wait and see game, but when do you think she may wake up again? I'd like one of the family to be here to reassure her when that happens."

"I thought you said you understand. Patience, my boy, patience. Others are asking the same questions, nurses, even the cleaning people have taken an interest and are asking that same question. Truth is, I don't know when, and we may not know any more after she wakes up. It may be she won't remember anything, or it maybe she will not be willing to answer questions about it. You should be prepared for that. I tell you again, now get out of here and get some rest. You look worse than seven miles of bad roads with the bridges out."

"I just don't want her to be here alone when she comes to again."

"If she wakes enough to know where she is, she can push the button and a nurse will be in here quicker than a cat can blink its eye. Believe me, they are all waiting for the time she will push that button and ring that bell. Once more I say go home, Dan. Get some rest." Dr. Tilford picked up his bag and headed for the door. Looking back over his shoulder, he said, "There's nothing you can do here. I'll talk to you tomorrow."

While the doctor stood at the nurses' station writing his report on Trudy's chart, Daniel's brother Larry was walking past. When he saw Dr. Tilford he stopped to inquire, "Any news today, Doctor?"

"She opened her eyes and said a few words. That's a good sign, but we just have to wait and see what happens next." Then pushing his glasses to the top of his head he sighed, "Larry, I'm concerned that Dan is getting too involved in this thing. I know at first he felt some responsibility because she fell in front of his store, but now we think there is a possibility that she was mugged." He whispered, "That's not for publication yet, but while she was awake that short time she told Daniel that her briefcase is missing, and apparently she was carrying a handbag. As you know, no handbag and no briefcase were found on or near her when you people found her. Dan said the only thing found at the scene was those hideous, big black, horned-rimmed glasses."

"You can count on me, Doctor; mum's the word. You worry me, Doctor, what do you mean, by 'too involved'?"

"He is taking far too much responsibility with this thing. I'm beginning to think he actually fancies himself in love with the girl. Try to discourage that sort of thing, will you? For all we know, she may be involved in something illegal, even dangerous."

"Oh, Doctor, I think you are being a little dramatic now."

"Still, my advice for all concerned is to take it slow and easy until we find out more about her; who she is, where she comes from, what she is doing in El Paso. If someone wanted that briefcase, who knows why, what might be in it?"

"A point well taken, Doctor. I'll go in and see how Dan is doing. He has been here since noon. Cynthia and I closed the store an hour ago; I can stay for a while. I'll do my best to send him home. If he thinks she is about to wake up, he'll be hard to keep away."

When Larry entered the room he saw Daniel sitting in a chair in the corner. He was leaning over, his elbows resting on his knees, his head held in his hands. When he looked up and saw Larry he started nervously running his fingers through his hair.

"What's with the roses, Dan? Looks like a dozen long stemmed yellow ones."

"You recall that on one side of her necklace is the name Trudy, on the other side is engraved a rose; that's why we call her Trudy Rose instead of the usual Jane Doe. In view of that fact, I imagine she is partial to roses. I think it will be nice for her to wake up to a nice big bouquet of them, don't you? And since this is Texas, I naturally thought of yellow ones; 'Yellow Rose of Texas,' you know."

Larry tried not to grimace at that last remark and ignored it. "I saw Dr. Tilford in the hall. He gave me the news about Trudy waking up for a while. He says that's a good sign."

"I know it's a good sign, but not good enough. Coming in here day after day, watching that intravenous dripping into her vein and not knowing how long it'll be before she wakes up permanently, if ever, is getting to me, and the thought that they are going to put a feeding tube in her stomach is making me sick."

"A feeding tube?"

"They say they'll have to do that if she doesn't wake up enough to take nourishment soon, like by the weekend."

"Feeding tube making you sick? How much good do you think you will be to her if you become ill?"

"You know what I mean. Not physically sick."

"Emotionally sick can be just as debilitating as physically sick. Go home,"

Larry admonished. "And on the way, stop for a haircut and shave. I don't want to see you back here looking like a bum. What will she think if she wakes up to find a shaggy haired, bleary-eyed man standing by her bed? The way you look now you'll scare the poor girl into apoplexy. No wonder she went back to sleep when she saw you," he grinned mischievously at his younger brother. "Better she should open her eyes to see a handsome, neatly turned out gentleman, such as me, beside her bed. I wouldn't mind being thought of as a knight in shining armor for a change."

"Okay, okay. All of us know you are a tall, dark-haired, dark-eyed wonder, but somehow I think she would prefer me, the one who has been keeping watch over her as she has been recuperating. I'll be back to check on her later. Tell her that for me, if she wakes up."

"It won't be necessary for you to come back, Dan. I'll be here for a while. And listen up, little brother; don't you think you are getting carried away with the idea that you owe this girl something because the incident happened in front of your store or do you just like the idea of being Joe Hero? Doc thinks you're getting too interested, too attached to her, maybe even attracted is a better word. I agree with him. You know nothing about her. I feel very strongly about that now that I know about the briefcase being taken."

"As I told Dr. Tilford, I realize that I know nothing about her, but she has no one here to care for her. Common decency dictates that we do what we can. I know what you are thinking, but as I also told Dr. Tilford, I can handle whatever happens."

"Just be careful, don't let your emotions get out of hand here. That's all I ask. There could be some physical risk to this thing as well. We don't know what she was carrying in that briefcase, or who is involved."

"Yes, big brother," Daniel sighed. "I hear you."

"Go on now. Get out of here, and don't forget what I told you about a haircut and shave."

"All right. All right. I'm going. I just wish you and Doc would butt out; you're starting to get on my nerves."

"What do you think you are doing to our nerves?"

Daniel stopped at the nurses' station on his way out. "Please leave a note in Trudy's file to call me if there is any change in her condition; call me at home or at the store. You have both numbers."

The nurse just looked at him, unsmiling. He wondered what she was thinking, same as all the others most likely. Probably thinks I am some kind of boob.

COME SEPTEMBER

On his way to the Upper Valley where he lived in the family home with his mother, he felt that someone was following him. He made a few unnecessary turns in hopes of losing anyone who might be tailing him. Nobody turned after him; he figured it was safe to go home.

Chapter 3

Daniel awoke the next morning feeling refreshed; there was new hope about Trudy's complete recovery. After all, he reasoned, even Dr. Tilford said her waking for a while was a good sign, and he certainly hadn't shown that much optimism up to that point. Daniel sat up in bed and looked into the dresser mirror across the room. The visage of a very unkempt young man stared back at him. He shook his head, a rueful grin on his face. *I'd pass for a man of forty-five any day in the week. Larry is right. I'll stop by the barbershop on my way to the store this morning.* Remembering what Larry told him about Trudy waking up to a disheveled man, he showered, shaved, and put on a new white shirt with a button-down collar. A glint of red showed through in his freshly shampooed blond hair. *The red tie with blue stripes will go well.* He topped it all off with a navy blue suit that fit his solid, well-built frame nicely.

He hurried down stairs, stopped in the kitchen and kissed his mother's cheek before sitting down to a plate of bacon and eggs, which he ate with gusto. "Son, I am happy to see you enjoy your breakfast." His eyes were bright with life for a change.

"I'm feeling good today, Mom. I'm encouraged about how Trudy is coming along. See you tonight."

"Call me if you need me today, son," she called to him as he backed his car past the kitchen door where she stood waving to him. A worried frown creased her forehead. "Please, God, take care of my boy. This whole thing is just too mysterious."

Arriving at the store, Daniel turned on the lights, put his briefcase on the shelf under the counter, and prepared for business of the day. Cash in the till and things in order, he pulled a step stool out and began shelving the books that had been delivered just before closing the night before. The shrill ringing of the phone interrupted his work. "Dan, Dr. Tilford here. I thought you'd like to know. In making my rounds this morning I noticed Trudy's eyelids quiver, then opened for about thirty seconds; it was obvious she was trying to open them. Now don't get your hopes up too high, but that is a very good sign."

"Whoopee! Maybe this is the turning point. Thanks for calling."

Two hours later, Daniel was walking briskly down the hall toward room 447, carrying a container of coffee, the morning paper and a book under his arm. One of the young nurses called out to him, "My, you're looking chipper this morning, Mr. Lindsey."

"Good morning," he answered. "Is it all right if I go in now?"

"Yes, she has been made ready for the day. She's looking good this morning, more color in her cheeks than usual."

I knew it. I knew it. Today is the day. But the day passed uneventfully, as did the next. He expressed disappointment that they had resorted to the feeding tube. "I hoped they could avoid that," he told Nurse Abigail.

Nurse Abigail, in her usual no-nonsense way, assured him that it was necessary. "It had to be done. You can see how much better her color is now that she is getting proper nourishment. Listen to me, young man; you just let the doctor take care of her medical needs. You just be here when she wakes up." By now the staff was beginning to take a real personal interest in Trudy's welfare.

The next morning soon after Daniel sat down in the chair across the room from Trudy's bed, he took the lid off his Styrofoam coffee beaker, poured cream into it from the little round container and stirred. Soon after, he settled back and unfolded his morning paper. He started to read while drinking his mid-morning coffee; he heard a low moan. Turning to look at her, he saw that she had raised her left arm to cover her eyes. He rushed to her side. "Is the light too bright?" He was disappointed that there was no response. He turned the overhead light off and took her hand is his. "Is that better?" Still there was no answer, just another moan as she turned her head toward him. *An encouraging sign,* he thought. He was happy she had heard his voice and that she was aware of the bright light shining on her eyelids. He felt a slight movement of her fingers, as if trying to squeeze his hand.

"Trudy, Trudy. Do you hear me?" She made no sound, but he felt another squeeze, a little stronger than before. He gently patted her hand. "I turned the bright light off; try to open your eyes."

She blinked rapidly a few times. He got a glimmer of her green eyes again before she clenched her lids closed; the eyes were green with golden flecks. He kept holding her hand, all the time speaking soothingly to her. "Trudy, can you open your eyes and talk to me? Please try. I'm Dan. I'm a friend."

"I, I know. I heard you, but I thought I was dreaming," her voice was hesitant and hoarse.

Finally, we're getting somewhere. He didn't call a nurse this time. He thought if they came running in they might scare her. He wanted to keep her talking if he could. Nurse Abigail be damned.

'Trudy, is your name Trudy?" No answer, so he kept talking to her. "Where do you live?" No answer. "What are you doing in El Paso?" He waited. "Where were you going the morning you fell?"

"Mugged," she said. "Book store."

"You were going to a book store? Were you going to The Bookmark Bookstore?" It stood to reason, he thought, if she was going to a bookstore and it happened in front of his store…*Probably a salesperson*, he thought. His heart felt lighter than it had since the incident. Probably no big mystery after all.

Her head moved slightly forward. *So that is where she was going.* He watched as she sighed and closed her eyes again. *Well, that's enough for now. I'll let her rest.*

He was elated at the turn of events and couldn't wait to ring his mother, but he didn't ring Dr. Tilford. He was mindful of the fact that he might not be able to keep him from telling the police. His joy soon vanished, however, when she murmured, "Come September." She hardly stirred in bed as she repeated, "Come September."

Now he was uneasy. *What could that mean? Could it be a code word? Was she to meet someone there, perhaps leave a message in a certain book for a cohort to find? Could his brother and Dr. Tilford's concerns be justified?* No, he would not believe it. He would tell no one. If the police knew what she said they would take it and run with it; no telling what they would try to make of it. Probably call in the FBI, maybe even make a federal case of it and call in the CIA. The fact that she remembered something, even if it was that she was mugged, even if *Come September was a code word it is encouraging,* he thought. *It meant something, meant she most likely would regain her full memory in time. I will not tell them she said come September. She is not well enough to go through questioning. I'll let her rest for a while.* He walked out of the room and down the hall to a waiting room and called Dr. Tilford. Daniel told him only that Trudy had blinked her eyes, and mumbled and moved her arm. "And I could see that the light bothered her eyes. That means she is becoming aware of her surroundings. Doesn't it?"

"Yes, it's a good sign. I was just leaving to make rounds, I'll be there in ten minutes."

"I'm in the small waiting room at the end of the hall. Meet me here," Daniel replied.

"Fine. Just hold on till I get there. We have to talk."

The doctor walked jauntily into the room where Daniel was, pulled a chair up in front of him and sat down. Facing him he looked him directly in the eye. "You'll have to tell the police that she's waking up. You know that, don't you?"

"Not yet," Daniel answered. "Please, let's let her get better before they start badgering her about what happened. I don't want them questioning her before she has all her faculties about her."

"Let me tell you something, Dan. You cannot protect this girl forever. Sooner or later you have to back off and let the authorities take over."

"Again, Doc, I'm asking you as a friend—"

Dr. Tilford interrupted, "Dan, I am your friend, but I am also this young lady's doctor; at your request, I might add. That said, I am alerting the authorities that she is showing signs of coming out of the coma. I'm sorry, Dan, but it has to be done. I'll do what I can to get them to wait until she is more alert to question her."

"Thank you," said Daniel. "I'll dance at your wedding with a cow bell on," he chuckled.

"Never mind. I'm not inviting you," he chuckled, and then gave him a weary look. "I'm going to look in on my patient now." He turned and left the room.

Daniel returned to the store around five o'clock that afternoon to find the place abuzz with business. After Cynthia rang up the last sale and all the customers left the store, she asked Daniel how the day went with Trudy. "I'm encouraged," he told her. "She opened her eyes briefly and there was slight movement of her fingers when I held her hand."

Held her hand? Cynthia said, "That's good, but Dan, I want to caution you—"

"I don't want to hear it, Cynthia. I've heard it from the doctor, I've heard it from Larry, and I've heard it from Mom. Please, try not to worry and just wish Trudy well. Anything else can wait."

With that outburst from Daniel, Cynthia thought it best to change the subject. "I didn't have time to finish shelving the books. Do you want me to stay and help you get it done?"

"Go on home to your family, Cynthia. You've done enough for the day. I want you to know I appreciate your help during this time. Give my love to the children and tell Albert that I hope everything will be back to normal soon and you can go back to your regular part-time hours here at the store."

"Albert doesn't mind my putting in extra time to help you out. The children are well cared for by Nanny Belle, and I am always home in time to help see to their homework and dinner."

"All the same, I know it has been inconvenient, to say the least. I want to apologize for my display of impatience. I know all of you are only concerned with my welfare."

"It's all right. I understand." Cynthia kissed her brother on the cheek. " See you tomorrow, Grumpy," she teased. She leaned her tall, supple body over and retrieved her bag from under the counter. Straightening, she pulled out a small compact, brushed a powder puff quickly over her nose, and run a lipstick over her lips. Her eyes twinkled as she snapped the compact shut. "Not bad for a thirty-five-year-old," she smiled as she returned it to her bag.

Daniel couldn't let that pass without comment. "You're darn betcha, sis. You are darn good-looking for your advanced age."

"Ha, ha, very funny." She walked to the door, opened it and before stepping out, turned and said, "Just for that, Little bro, here's to you." She gave him a thumbed nose and a big smile.

"That's my sister, always has the last word," he called to her as she headed out the door.

Daniel watched her as she hurried out onto Mesa Street and climbed into her maroon Datsun and drove away. He thought how lucky he was to have such a loving and helpful family. *I just wish they wouldn't be so concerned about Trudy; about where she came from, what she's doing here, that she will bring trouble to me. Of course, I am frustrated in my effort to find out more about Trudy, but I don't need all these questions.*

He opened the half-empty box of books and started stacking them on a cart, alphabetizing by the author's name. *I see Cynthia finished with the L's before she left.* He often mumbled aloud as he shelved books in alphabetical order according to the authors' name, "Ma, Mi, Mo. Morgan. Trudy Morgan?" He looked at the title on the book cover, *Come September.* Ah-ha, That's it. *Come September.* Of course, she knew her book would be out soon and she came to arrange a book signing or to otherwise promote the sale. This revelation made him so happy he couldn't wait to tell the doctor, his family, and anyone else who would listen. He turned the book over to read the blurb about the author on the dust cover. The biography was scant. Not much there. *I'll call the publishing house.* He was eager to find out about this mysterious author, Trudy Morgan.

After calling the publisher, his next call was to Dr. Tilford. "Great news. I think I know what Trudy was doing in the area the morning of the incident. In fact I'm sure I know."

"Tell me about it."

"First off, I now know her full name, Trudy Morgan. She is the author of a book titled *Come September*. That clears up the mystery of why she said those words while momentarily waking out of her coma, deep sleep, whatever you want to call it."

"What words?"

"Oh, that's right, I didn't tell you, did I? She mumbled the words 'come September' a day or two ago while I was visiting her."

"No, I don't believe you did tell me. What else did you not tell me?"

"Nothing else."

"Just a minute, where did you get this bit of information?"

"While shelving books from a box of samples this morning, I found a novel written by her. Her name is on the dust jacket. So you see, the police can call off their dogs, no great mystery. They can just concentrate on finding the robber."

"Whoa, not so fast; is her picture on the dust jacket?"

"Yes. It's not a good likeness; those big horned-rim glasses practically cover her face, but I can tell it is her."

"That is good news, explains one part of the puzzle. I would still like to know why someone hit her; why they didn't just grab her handbag if it was a simple robbery."

"Let's not create a whole new mystery surrounding what happened. I don't want to give the police fodder for an investigation into what she was doing here when it is perfectly obvious to me that she was here to promote her book."

"Still...?"

"What?"

"You should be able to learn a lot from the biography on the dust jacket."

"Not so much, I'm afraid. It states only that this is a first novel by the author, that she is also a freelance writer, and that she lives on an island in Puget Sound off the state of Washington."

"Puget Sound? Which island?"

" It doesn't give that information, just an island in Puget Sound."

"Wonder why not? There are 172 islands and reefs in Puget Sound. Where can we find her freelance writing?"

"It's just a short bio, very few details about her personal history. It doesn't even say in which publications her freelance writing is published."

"I see." Daniel could just picture Dr. Tilford rubbing his chin, frown lines creasing his forehead, like always, when he was concerned about a problem. Dr. Tilford sounded more worried than ever. "That is unusual; sounds like there may be some reason that she doesn't want to give much away about herself or where she lives. Could mean there is a reason for that. We may be protecting a fugitive."

Chapter 4

Daniel tried to sound unconcerned. He chuckled, "Oh, not to worry. She's probably in a witness protection program."

"No joke, Dan, I don't like it. I don't believe I've ever read the biography of an author on a dust jacket that didn't give more information than that, and there is usually a very good picture there along with it, most of the time flattering. Did you think about calling her publisher? I'm sure they will have more information than what is on the dust cover."

Daniel still persisted in trying to sound unconcerned. "Come now, Doc, I was joking. Why on earth would an author be in a witness protection program?" He didn't want to admit that he had already called her publishing house and was told that she was a very private person and that she insisted on keeping her privacy.

"It's happened before, Dan. A journalist could find out something unsavory about a person or persons while investigating a story, someone finds out what she knows and wants to quiet her. It sounds serious. For her own safety I think we have no choice, we must inform the police about the book and about the lack of information about the author on the dust jacket."

"Please, I'm asking you not to make a federal case of it. I'm sure if the mugger wanted to kill her he, or maybe she, would have accomplished their goal, and if your scenario is right, they obviously found what they were looking for or they would have shown up again by now."

Dr. Tilford made a grumbling sound. "But what if they didn't find it and are just waiting for an opportunity to get at her? Maybe the culprit thought he hit her hard enough to kill her. It does take quite a blow to put a person in a coma for such a long time. When he, or they, find out she is alive her life could be in danger, especially if they didn't find what they were looking for. Even if they did, and they discover she is showing signs of coming out of the coma, they may try again; they may want to protect themselves from what they found out she knows. After all, she can't give out information while she is in a coma. Her awakening may be what they are waiting for."

"I have to admit I hadn't thought of it in that light. Aw, but we are probably making a mountain where a molehill is more in order."

"Are you willing to bet her life on it?"

"Well, no. You're right. I better ask to have a cot moved into her room so I can be there at night."

"You are a dreamer, Dan. Do you realize how absurd that sounds? The hospital won't allow such a thing. You aren't a relative, blood or otherwise. The chance of you getting permission for that is absolutely nil. Anyway, what could you do? Forget it."

"I could be a deterrent."

"Don't be silly, Dan. You could get yourself killed; that's what you could do." With that he turned and left Daniel standing there wondering if the doctor was right. Maybe it would be safer to tell the police about the book and lack of information available about the author.

An hour later a phone call from Dr. Tilford. "Dan, can you come over to my office? I'd like to speak to you in person about a few things."

When Daniel arrived at the doctor's office he found him giving instructions to an assistant. Immediately after the assistant left the room the doctor spoke, "I don't want to worry you, Dan, but the witness protection program might be the best thing we can hope for here. Not to belabor the point, Dan, but we don't know, it's possible she's a criminal hiding from the law. That whole privacy thing sounds fishy to me. I'm telling you, Dan, I'm not waiting any longer to tell the police about everything we know. Do you want me to report what you found out, or rather didn't find out, to the police or do you want to call them?"

"You can do it," Daniel sighed. He felt dejected. "Do that, but do me a favor and ask for Lieutenant Mackey. I've known him for a long time. From all accounts he is a square shooter, good as his word and all that. In the meantime I think I'll ask a few questions around the hospital; find out if they've seen any unaccounted for strangers hanging around."

"Dan, I don't think that is wise. Just leave it to the law."

As soon as Daniel left, Dr. Tilford hurried to the telephone and called the local police. "Lieutenant Mackey, please."

"May I say who is calling?"

"Doctor Tilford. Make haste." He felt there was no time to waste.

"Lieutenant Mackey here. What can I do for you, Doctor?"

"We may have a bit of a break in the Miss Trudy Rose case." The lieutenant was all ears.

Dr. Tilford told him everything he knew about it. The doctor told him about the dust jacket on the book Daniel found, and gave him the details of the lack of information about the author. "What do you make of it, Lieutenant? Don't you think you should place a guard outside her door, just in case there might be foul play involved?"

"Interesting. We'll have to see what develops. We can't assign a guard for her unless we have more to go on than what we know so far. I'll do some snooping, talk to the chief and see what I come up with."

"You can't afford not to provide protection for this woman, Lieutenant. If anything happens to her, the press will have the police department for lunch." Dr. Tilford was dead serious.

"Okay, okay, I'll do my best."

"That's all I can ask. However, I do think there is reason for concern."

Lieutenant Mackey asked, "Has something happened that we don't know about?"

"I've told you all there is to tell."

"As I said, Doctor, we'll look into it. In the meantime, sit tight and let us handle it."

"That's all right with me, but I don't know how Dan will handle it. I'm sure you read the article in the paper about how the owner of the store where she fell has taken an interest in seeing that she is cared for, feeling some responsibility for her welfare because she fell in front of his store."

"I did see the article. Damn fool. Dan always was a do-gooder; I've known him since high school."

"In my opinion it is more than a casual interest; he's acting more like a lover than a Good Samaritan. He asks that you be in charge of the investigation. He trusts you. Can you handle the case, Lieutenant?"

"That's up to the chief, Doctor. I'll ask for the assignment. That's all I can do."

"I do hope you can do something before Dan does something foolish, like trying to find out more on his own. I tell you, the man is getting almost irrational."

"Get a handle on him, Doctor. We can't have a loose cannon running around messing up the investigation."

"I'll do my best, Lieutenant."

Back at the store Daniel was eager for closing time to come. He turned out the lights, walked out the back door, and headed for his car. Driving the speed limit along Oleander Street, he slowed down as he passed the park. He wanted to get a good look at the man in a parked car; why would anyone be sitting in a parked car, facing the road, this time of night? He thought about turning around and going back to the store. He couldn't remember locking the back door as he rushed out. *I'll worry about that later.*

He was relieved the next morning to find that he had locked the door to the store the night before. "I must be going nuts, I don't remember locking it. Besides that, I'm starting to talk to myself."

That evening he walked into the hospital just in time to see a dark haired, dark-skinned man turning away from the nurses' station. He hurried over to the desk and asked, "Who was that? What did he want?"

Susan, the nurse on desk duty, looking at him kindly said, "Mr. Lindsey, I'm sorry but I'm not sure I should give you that information."

"He just looks familiar. That's all." *Thank goodness, I don't have to deal with Nurse Abigail tonight. Susan is a sweet girl, much easier to deal with than Madam Abigail.*

Susan continued, "As I said, I'm not sure I should give you that information, but it's not surprising that he looks familiar to you. He's a city councilman, represents the Lower Valley. Well, I guess it's no secret; I can tell you. I'm sure it'll be in the paper tomorrow morning; his wife is having a baby here tonight." Then she added, "Your friend in 447 has been restless today, mumbling something unintelligible."

"Thanks, Susan." He hurried down the hall looking at everyone lingering there, wondering if this one might be there to do harm to Trudy. It could even be a nurse. It's not impossible that someone could be placed here as an employee of the hospital in order to have access to her, maybe know when she comes out of the coma, or worse, see that she doesn't. He looked across the hallway. Who is that man over there hiding behind a newspaper? He tried to shake off the uneasiness he felt. I must control these jitters, get hold of myself. I can't go around suspicious of everyone who comes into this hospital just because I don't know them.

When he entered the room he was not surprised, considering what Susan said, to see that Trudy was making small, restless movement with her head and flailing around with her arms. He took her hands in his. "Trudy, Trudy, can you hear me?" Her eyelids blinked rapidly. *Is she trying to answer me or is it just wishful thinking on my part?* he wondered.

Moving her head from side to side, she murmured, at first incoherently; he thought she said something about lights and jewels. *Why would she be carrying jewelry? She pulled a heist? No, I won't believe it. Jewelry salesperson. No, she is a writer.*

"Tell me about the jewels. Were there many jewels in your briefcase?"

"In my briefcase?" She hesitated, "No, no jewels in briefcase."

"Where were the jewels?" No answer. I'll ask her another time, a time when she is alert.

Chapter 5

Finally the time came when Trudy opened her eyes wide and spoke in a slow monotone, asking again, "Where am I? Oh, I remember. I'm in a hospital in El Paso, Texas."

"Trudy, that's right, you are in a hospital in El Paso. You are not to worry, you are safe here." *I hope that is true.*

"What did you call me?"

"Trudy. You are Trudy Morgan, aren't you?"

She hesitated, "Trudy? Trudy, you say?" She seemed to remember something; "Yes, yes, I am Trudy Morgan." She seemed to panic. "Why am I here? Oh, I know, I was mugged."

"Right. I believe you are here to promote your book, *Come September*." It was obvious she was hazy about what happened when she was awake for the short time before.

"Oh, I think you told me that before."

"Yes, but I don't expect you to remember everything I told you while you were half asleep. Do you recall having an accident outside a bookstore on Mesa Street?"

"I don't know. I'm tired. Let me think. Are you a doctor?" Her words came slow and a little slurred as if her tongue was too large for her mouth.

"I'm not a doctor. My name is Dan. I'm the owner of the book store where your accident happened."

"I see. Will you please let me rest?" Her eyes closed again.

"Wait a minute, Trudy. Try to stay awake one more minute." He slapped the inside of her wrist. "Do you remember speaking to me before, a day or two ago?"

"A day or two ago?" She opened her eyes and seemed to be focusing better than before. "How long have I been here? Have I missed the release date of my book?"

"You did, but don't worry, your agent has taken care of everything. I took the liberty of calling your publishing house. Don't look so concerned, Miss Trudy Rose. They swore me to secrecy before they gave me the name and telephone number of your agent; something about your whereabouts had to be kept a secret. Your agent was beside himself wondering what had happened to you; now he knows where you are and that you have been in a coma. He claims to know nothing about why you were mugged." *I think he doth protest too loud.*

That look of panic again. She mumbled, "No, no one must know where I am."

"Listen to me, Trudy. Your agent made it very clear that I must not divulge where you are, that your safety depends on my word. However, someone knows where you are, otherwise why did they take your briefcase? That's why the local police are keeping a guard outside your door twenty-four hours a day. Trudy, I'm sorry, but Dr. Tilford, your doctor, insisted on calling in the local police. It is for your safety."

"Guard outside my door?"

"Yes, the police think it best, and I agree with them. I had to ask for their protection for your safety. Do you understand?"

She looked puzzled for a minute. "Yes, all right, I do understand. Uh-huh." She seemed unconcerned about it now. "My briefcase. Oh, right. I remember they took my briefcase and my purse. It was not an accident; it was a mugging, or robbery," she hastened to add. "Wait. Wait. Did you say police? No FBI?"

"Are we playing twenty questions here?" Daniel thought his remark about the police didn't register with her; he could see he was wrong. He tried to sound jovial. "'Don't worry. Your agent was very explicit on that too, 'No FBI' he said. That's okay; the local boys don't like the FBI poking their noses in anyway, at least not until they are ready to invite them to do so." He wondered why no FBI, but he had given his word and would honor it until otherwise permitted to change it, or until it was out of his ability to control. *I will do my best to keep the police from bringing in the Feds.* He walked into her bathroom; quietly closing the door behind him, threw cold water on his face, dried off, and went back outside to call Dr. Tilford. "Doctor Tilford, Trudy's color is improving."

He was delighted with Dr. Tilford's reaction. "We're on our way now, Dan. Sit tight. Things are looking up."

At home that night, Daniel went to bed early, but slept fitfully. Morning came before he was ready for it. The shrill sound of the ringing telephone startled him. He picked up the receiver from the phone on his bedside table, "Yes?"

"This is Lieutenant Mackey."

Daniel became instantly alert. He didn't have time to analyze his emotions—fear or joy? *It must be important, the lieutenant calling so early in the morning.* He was silent, waiting for the news, good or bad. He exhaled a breath of relief when he heard, "Dan, we have a briefcase that was turned in by a Hallmark card store owner. It was found in the store dumpster about a month or so ago. The store owner just put it under the counter and forgot about it. He didn't think about the importance of it until one of his helpers lost a bracelet and was checking the lost-and-found column in the *El Paso Times*. She saw a number to call if a briefcase was found. It's nice dark brown sealskin. We're wondering if it could be the one taken from Miss Morgan. The chief is now taking a personal interest in the case. He doesn't like to be outdone by a crook."

"I hope that is good news, but I don't like the idea of a notice being put in the paper. That could alert the wrong people as to where she is."

"Nothing to worry about there; it was just a simple notice in the lost-and-found with instructions to call a certain number if found. A policewoman answering as Sally answered the telephone at that number. No indication that it was a police number. Sally went out and picked up the briefcase acting as if it were a personal item. But it's no secret where Miss Morgan is. You know an article appeared in the paper when she first took the fall reporting the incident; it named the hospital at that time."

"I know, but it's good they don't know it was a police woman who called. Whew, thank heaven. You are a clever guy, Lieutenant."

"I have to be to be an effective detective; all detectives are clever, that's how we get our man," he chuckled.

"Was anything found in the briefcase, any fingerprints or other evidence on or in it?" Daniel asked.

"We're looking into that now, but we didn't find anything inside and chances are slim that we will be able to lift any clear fingerprints from it considering how long it may have been in that dumpster and the way it has been handled since it was found, but if we do we'll send them to Washington for identification. They are dusting it for fingerprints as we speak."

"Sounds good, Lieutenant Mackey. Trudy is showing some signs that she may really be coming out of the coma. Keep in touch. I'll let you know if she does and I can get a description of the briefcase from her. I will appreciate your cooperation in not trying to question her too soon, and I want to thank you for keeping the details, her name and all, out of the paper. And please, don't get the Feds in on this."

"Why are you so adamant about that, Dan?"

"I have my reasons." He didn't tell the lieutenant about Trudy mumbling, "No FBI," with a frightened look on her face. "Just please don't do it."

"I hear you." Daniel noticed no promise, just "I hear you." He plunked the receiver down on the cradle and bounced out of bed, ran into the bathroom and turned on the shower. After dressing he took the stairs two steps at a time. His mother had grapefruit, coffee, and a bowl of oatmeal waiting for him.

As she waited for the toast to pop up, she scolded, "Son, I wish you wouldn't gobble your food; it's not good for you."

"I know, Mom, but I'm in a hurry this morning." He told her about the police finding the briefcase.

"I understand, but eating fast will not help the situation; it will only give you indigestion. Only time will tell what's going on with Trudy."

As soon as he finished his breakfast, he pulled on his navy blazer, grabbed his briefcase, and kissed his mother's cheek. "You are a dear, Mom, for helping me so much with the store, and Cynthia has been a jewel." Rushing out the door he jumped into his car and drove to the hospital.

On entering room 447 he found nurses hovering around Trudy's bed. He was frightened until he saw that Trudy was sitting up in bed. But then he noticed that she was not opening her eyes.

"What's wrong?" he rushed to Trudy's side.

"Nothing is wrong; we think just the opposite," Nurse Abigail chortled. "We are just trying to get her awake. She was restless during the night; the doctor ordered a sedative for her. That may be why she is sleeping soundly. We want to change her bed and get her ready for the day, and besides she is stirring around; seems to be trying to say something. Here, sir, you take over; she may respond better to you." With that she motioned for the other nurses to leave the room with her.

"Trudy, wake up. I think your briefcase has been found. Can you wake up and tell me what color it is?"

She squirmed around in bed before she answered; her words were still slurred. "Sure, sure," she said, "I think...."

"That's all right, Trudy. Just try to open your eyes." He went into the bathroom, wet a couple of washcloths with cold water, and applied one to her forehead. With the other he swabbed the inside of her elbows and wrists.

She did manage to open her eyes and she looked at the tubes that invaded her body. "Oh no," she murmured. Closed her eyes tight again.

"I'm turning the bright light off, Trudy, hear the click; open your eyes."

Dr. Tilford came in shortly after she woke up. Daniel told him what happened. The doctor took her wrist in his hand, feeling for her pulse beat. "That's very good, young lady. It tells us you are getting better." Turning to Daniel, he whispered, "It looks like her total recognition of what is going on will be a slow process. Hang in there, fellow. All of this is good news."

Daniel knew the doctor was right, but he was impatient. He didn't want to leave her, but he had to open the store. "I'll see you tonight, Trudy Rose."

She raised her hand as if trying to wave.

He heard the phone ringing when he entered the store and rushed to answer it. An unpleasant voice on the line barked, "What's the deal, stupid? Why are you so interested in the broad? Expecting a little something when and if she wakes up? Well, I can save you some trouble; if you keep meddling she ain't gonna, and if you want to stay healthy you better quit, butt out. You don't know who you're fooling with."

"Listen, asshole...." Before Daniel could say more the receiver on the other end was banged down so hard it stunned his eardrum.

He called Cynthia to come to the store as soon as possible. "Make it quick, sis, I have to go down to the police station." Cynthia didn't question him. She knew it was important or he wouldn't have called her to come in without giving her more notice. She was walking in the store twenty minutes later. Daniel didn't take time to explain. "Sorry, sis, no time to talk."

He rushed past her and ran out the backdoor, jumped into his red Thunderbird and headed to police headquarters. He told the lieutenant about the phone call. "I'm scared, Lieutenant Mackey. This means they are still watching and probably know she is beginning to show signs of recovery. Maybe they even heard about the briefcase being found."

"We're on top of the thing, Dan. I'll inform the boys to be double diligent about watching the hospital, especially the fourth floor where she is."

As Daniel was getting into his car, he felt that someone was watching him. *My imagination is getting the better of me.* Satisfied that the lieutenant's boys were keeping a watchful eye on Trudy, he returned to the store to relieve Cynthia.

"Cynthia, please go by the house on your way home and tell Mom to keep the doors locked, and to be sure Tiger is in the house with her except when he has to go outside or when she takes him for a walk."

"Has something happened that you aren't telling us about?"
"Not really."
"Then why should Mom have Tiger in the house with her?"
"Tiger is a good watchdog. After all, he is a German shepherd; his bark and ferocious looks would scare an intruder, they won't know it's all bluster and no action. Anyway, it's just a precaution. You know how many robberies there has been in the El Paso area recently." He didn't tell her about the threatening phone call; he didn't want her to worry unduly, and he didn't want his mother to know about it unless she had to.

Cynthia's quizzical look proved she didn't believe him. *She knows something is up, but I'm not telling her more.*

Daniel had some book work to do after he closed the store that night. By the time he had a bite to eat and drove to the hospital, visiting hours was almost over. As he walked from his car toward the hospital entrance, he shrugged off the feeling that someone was watching him again. He was rushing down the hall on the second floor when Nurse Abigail stopped him. "Mr. Lindsey, I have something to tell you. I wanted to tell you what happened today."

Daniel froze. "What, what happened?" He didn't know what to expect.

Chapter 6

"Mr. Lindsey," Nurse Abigail smiled broadly. "Trudy was awake most of the day. I finally got her to talk to me; she wanted to know if a man had been talking to her while she slept. She wanted to know if it was a dream. She said it seemed so real. I assured her that it was real. She seems to be afraid of something. I told her that you would probably come by tonight and that she was not to worry, that you are a nice man and only want the best for her. She looked pleased at that. I knew you wouldn't want her to fret. Then she wanted to know if it was the same man who was here this morning. She seemed relieved when I told her you were one and the same."

"Thank you, that was thoughtful of you. Will it be all right for me to go in her room now? Maybe you should go with me, might make her feel safer if she is still awake. She seems to forget that we have talked from time to time."

"I don't think she will be forgetting from now on. She seems very alert today, but I'll be happy to go in with you."

They walked into Trudy's room together. Daniel was relieved to see that she was awake, and more alert than at any time before.

Abigail spoke to Trudy. "This is the young man who has been visiting you every day since your fall." The hospital staff still didn't know the full story of what had happened.

She opened her eyes and tried to focus on him. He went closer and said, "Trudy, I'm so happy you are feeling better. Do you remember the conversation we had earlier?"

"Trudy?" She looked puzzled. He thought it was due to her having been in a coma so long. He let it pass. Then in a low voice, she said, "Thank you…everything."

"You are very welcome, Trudy. You are getting so well we'll have to talk to the doctor about getting rid of some of these tubes." He saw a slight smile as she slid her hand on the bed toward him. He took it is his. She squeezed his fingers.

COME SEPTEMBER

Abigail saw that Trudy seemed at ease with Daniel. "Well, I can't stay in here all evening fooling with you kids," she kidded, as she walked out the door, closing it behind her.

Daniel said, "Trudy, do you remember telling me you had a briefcase that the mugger took from you?" She made a slight movement with her hand and nodded. "Can you tell me what color it is?"

"Color?" She hesitated. He thought she was going back to sleep. Finally she repeated, "Color?" After another pause she put her lips together and tried to speak. "Br, bro, brown."

"Brown?"

She nodded again.

"It's all right, Trudy. You can rest for a while now. I understand you have been quite active today. That's great."

The next afternoon when he entered her room he was surprised to see that she was sitting up again, and they had removed the feeding tube from her stomach. The only tube left was an intravenous in her arm. She was all cleaned up; her hair had been combed and pulled back from her face in a ponytail. She looked beautiful even in her hospital gown. He could see light brown roots next to her scalp, belying the very black ends. There was a pale pink on her lips. Nurse Abigail's handiwork, he suspected. *Abigail likes to act tough, but deep down she is a real pussycat.* "It's nice to see you looking so well," he smiled at her.

He made small talk to her for a while. "Have you been in El Paso before?"

"No," she even managed a little smile. "I feel better today."

"I'm glad to hear that." He told her about the weather in El Paso. "Dry climate out here. We're in the desert, you know." Anything he could think of to keep her attention, which he felt he was doing at least part of the time, better than anytime before. Then he eased into a few questions about where she lived, "Tell me, Trudy, where do you live?" She looked puzzled again. Where do your folks live?" No answer. "Do you have brothers and sisters?" She just looked at him with a confused frown.

I think she knows, I think she is just being secretive. But why? Okay, I'll try again later. *I'll ask her about something that won't cause her to feel threatened.* "Stay with me for a few minutes longer and then I'll leave you alone to rest. Let's talk about the jewels you spoke about. Where were they? Did someone take them from you?""

"I spoke about jewels?"

"Yes. One day when you were tossing about in bed, when you were still confused. Were they in your briefcase? Did someone take them from you?"

She shook her head from side to side and repeated, "I spoke about jewels? Oh, I remember. Lights like a whole world of jewels shining in the night. Beautiful jewels. Jewels in the valley, jewels on the mountain, jewels everywhere."

Now he was really puzzled. *Jewels in the valley? Jewels on the mountain? Ah ha! I've often heard people say that when they fly into the pass at night the lights look like jewels.* "Trudy, did you fly into El Paso at night?"

"El Paso at night? Yes. We flew in over the dark desert then suddenly, lights like jewels, like a mammoth bowl of sparkling jewels. It was a beautiful sight. I fell in love with El Paso right then. I want to see more of it."

"I agree, when I fly into El Paso at night I, too, am reminded of jewels twinkling in the dark night. It's quite a sight; we see the lights from El Paso as well as the many, many lights across the Rio Grande in Juarez."

"Juarez. I want to go to Juarez. But now I am tired."

"I know. You can rest now. When you are all better I'll take you to Juarez. We'll paint the town."

She smiled. "Paint the town. Good. What color shall we paint it?"

Oh she is feeling a little feisty; that's wonderful to see. "Well I'd say red, what do you think?"

Her smile is beautiful, he thought. When he said goodbye to her she looked like she wanted to say something, but no words were forthcoming. "Sleep well. I'll see you tomorrow." He kissed her forehead and left.

He drove only a few blocks when he thought he saw someone tailing him. He looked in his rearview mirror. *Not again. That's the blue Taurus I saw in the parking lot earlier, the same one in the park.* Upon arriving home he called the detective. "I'm sorry to bother you at home, Lieutenant Mackey. I just wanted to tell you that I got a few words out of Trudy today. She did say brown when I asked what color her briefcase was. She was much more lucid than ever, even a little witty."

"Good, good. It's quite all right to call me at home, Dan. I have an idea. I'll bring the briefcase in and show it to her now that she is feeling better and is more alert. Maybe she will recognize it, might even help her remember more of what happened before the accident. We lifted one fingerprint off the briefcase that doesn't match the prints of any of the people who work in the store where it was found. We sent it for identification, but have no results yet, but I expect to hear something soon. I'll bring the briefcase in tomorrow."

"That sounds like a winner to me. Goodnight, Lieutenant."

"Goodnight, Dan. Get some rest. I think we are on the homestretch."

Danie thought, *On the homestretch except for finding out who wanted her briefcase and why.*

The next night he stopped for dinner on his way home. *Who is that guy who came in here right after I did? Damned if he doesn't look familiar; that's the sucker I saw driving that blue Taurus, the one that was following me. It's time for a little evasive maneuvering.* He got up and casually walked to the men's washroom. After a couple of minutes he walked out and went into the kitchen.

"Manuel, I think I'm being followed. If that guy out there in the booth next to the door tries to follow me, detain him if you can. I don't want the SOB to know where I live." *He probably already knows.*

Manuel picked up the order he was waiting for with a flourish, turned around to face Daniel, "*Sí, Señor* Lindsey. I trép him, accidéntly of course; may spill a little hot chili con queso on him, accidéntly of course."

"Of course, accidentally, but don't do anything that will get you in trouble with your boss." He smiled, "Thanks, Manny." He ran out the back door, around to the side parking lot, jumped in his car and hurried away. He took several unnecessary turns on his way home to the Upper Valley, hoping to lose the blue Taurus if the occupant tried to follow.

Sleep didn't come easy. He kept thinking about Trudy and wondering if the police guard outside her door was keeping a sharp eye out for strangers. He was glad Cynthia would be in earlier than usual tomorrow. He could spend more time at the hospital.

When he walked into Trudy's room around 2 o'clock the following afternoon, he found her even more alert than she had been the day before. The intravenous was no longer attached to her arm. He saw a tray on her bedside table; on it was a cup containing some kind of broth. "Well, hello, Miss Trudy Rose. You're looking well today." He thought she was more beautiful than ever.

"Trudy? You keep calling me Trudy Rose."

"Yes, isn't that your name?" She said nothing, just seemed to be thinking. "That's the name on your book, Trudy Morgan, and there is a rose on one side of the pendent on your necklace. I just added that because I thought you must like roses, or maybe that's your middle name."

"The book, oh yes. The book." She spoke slowly, in a clear voice, choosing her words carefully. Then a cloud seemed to be lifted from her mind. "I have to trust somebody. I know I can trust you, Dan. Only you." She lifted her hand, taking hold of the front of his shirt. "My name...."

Just then Lieutenant Mackey came through the door carrying the briefcase in question. "Here we are, young lady. I hear you're feeling much better today. Do you feel like looking at this case? We think it could be the one taken from you the day of the mugging." He placed it on the bed beside her.

She closed her eyes, her eyelids pressed together tightly. Then her eyes began to open slowly. She looked at it, placed her hand on it, and moved it around, relishing the feel of the smooth cover. "I remember how carefree and happy I was the day I bought it in Vienna. Open it?" Lieutenant Mackey opened it and held it up so she could see inside. She nodded her head.

"I thought so." He looked pleased with himself. "Thank you." He snapped it shut and started to the door holding it in his left hand; he reached for the doorknob with his right.

Trudy became visibly alarmed. "No, no." She tried to reach out her arm but she didn't have enough strength. She had been sedentary and subsiding on liquids too long.

"I have to take it for safekeeping," the lieutenant said.

Again that frightened look, "No, no. Mine."

Daniel spoke up. "Lieutenant, could you possible leave it here for a while? Let's step outside for a minute." Once outside the room he whispered, "If you will leave it here I'll try to find out why she is so upset about you taking it away; I'll talk to her, try to get her to relax about it."

"Alright, but I'm holding you responsible, Dan. That is an important piece of evidence. I'll be back in an hour. I'll have to take it back to headquarters at that time, no ifs, ands or buts about it; I'll be taking it in. That is the only piece of evidence we have."

"Understood."

When Daniel was alone in the room with her he said, "Now, Trudy, why are you so upset about the lieutenant taking the case? He'll see that it's returned to you when the investigation is over."

"No FBI. Can't see inside the case."

The FBI is not involved. The local police are handling it, and I'm sure they have already looked inside it. Remember, Trudy, I told you the local police would not call in the FBI unless they have to."

"I forgot you told me no FBI." She hesitated. "Bottom out," she whispered. He looked at her, clearly puzzled. She looked around to be sure no one could hear. He could barely hear her whisper. "Secret bottom."

"I see." He looked inside but couldn't see that there was a secret bottom in the case. He took a Swiss Army knife out of his pocket, the one he used for opening boxes at the store. He slipped the blade between what appeared to be the bottom and the side of the case, pried it up, and sure enough, there was a false bottom. There it was, what she wanted him to find.

"What's this?"

"Diary, past year."

He started to put it next to her hand. She waved it away and shook her head to indicate that she didn't want to take it. "Please, you take, read it, hide it."

Chapter 7

"All right, Trudy, I understand. I know you are having a hard time knowing in whom you can trust, but I will do my best to protect you and let you know others I know you can trust. Do you understand what I'm telling you? You do trust me? Right?"

She nodded her head.

"Good," he said. *Whew, that's one more hurdle crossed.* He put the diary in his inside breast pocket, patted it and said, "I'll read it tonight." He thought he saw a slight smile cross her face; it was gone so quickly he wasn't sure.

Lieutenant Mackey came back for the briefcase in one hour just as he said he would. He stood outside the door out of sight of Trudy and motioned for Daniel to come out. "I'm going for a drink of water," Daniel told Trudy. "I'll be back shortly."

The lieutenant asked, "Did you find out why she was so reluctant to let me take the briefcase."

"Who knows? Just feeling insecure I guess. She is alright with it now." He felt guilty lying, but felt it the only thing he could do under the circumstances; he had promised Trudy that he wouldn't tell anyone about the diary unless she gave him the go-ahead. His explanation seemed to be satisfactory with the lieutenant. Daniel knew he could trust Lieutenant Mackey, but felt he would be betraying Trudy's trust if he told him about the diary without her permission, and too, he wanted to read the diary before the police got their hands on it. He hoped to make the lieutenant understand later. They walked back into the room together. The lieutenant picked up the briefcase and asked Trudy, "May I take it now?"

She looked at Daniel; he nodded his head. She answered in a clear voice, "Yes."

The look that passed between Daniel and Trudy was not lost on the lieutenant. *I see, Dan is the only one she trusts. I'll have to remember that in dealing with her, at least for now.*

The lieutenant seemed satisfied with the answer Daniel gave him. He smiled and waved to the two of them from the door. "See you later."

Daniel took her hand is his and gave it a little squeeze. He felt a movement in her fingers as she squeezed back, stronger than the last time, getting stronger every day. He leaned over her, pushed her hair back from her temple, and kissed her lightly on the cheek. "I have to go now Trudy Rose. I have some reading to do." He gave her a knowing look.

"Thanks." She seemed to relax. Then whispered, "Nonie Lee."

He smiled and patted her hand. "Nonie Lee? Who is Nonie Lee?"

She smiled and pointed to her chest.

Uh huh. That's why she had trouble answering to Trudy. "Nonie Lee? Is that your name?" Her nod told him it was. "That's a beautiful name. *The mystery deepens, he thought. Why Trudy? Maybe it's just a pen name, but since there are so many unknowns surrounding this whole thing, perhaps I'd better just stick with using Trudy Rose for the present.*

"Do you mind if I continue to call you Trudy Rose for now?"

"Trudy Rose, good."

He rushed home, ate the dinner his mother had prepared for him and excused himself. "Mind if I take my coffee upstairs, Mom? I have some reading to do." He rushed upstairs to his suite, turned on the floor lamp in his sitting room. settled into his brown leather recliner, and started to read Trudy Rose's diary. Nonie Lee? *I'll have to get used to this change, but it's Trudy Rose for a while yet.* He opened it to the first page. There he saw the first date was sixteen months earlier. He read:

> April 1
> Dear Diary,
> Tomorrow I'll no longer be me. It has been arranged for me to cease to exist as Nonie Lee Talbert, at least for some time to come. April 1, I'll be assigned a new name, a new home. Aw, April's Fool Day, what a coincidence! I hope I can fool them. When I disappear from the Washington scene the word will be passed around newsrooms that I am backpacking in Europe, aiming for a trip around the world before returning home. Only my agent, Hal Hollis, my attorney, Ed Thompson, and my mother and father and Rob will know this is not true. I'll miss my parents and friends, but my very life may be at stake. I'll spend the rest of today readying for my disappearance; changing type of clothes, my hairstyle and color;

glasses will be added, nice big black horn-rimmed ones should do the trick.

April 2
Dear Diary,
Mom and Dad were brave when I left them this morning. Their eyes were glossy with unshed tears, but they know I'll be safe where I'm going. They know I love them and that they will be in my prayers and thoughts even though I will not be able to contact them directly for a while, a long while. My dad's last words to me as I walked out the back door to meet Rob in the alley were, "My darling girl, we don't know where you're going, but our love will follow wherever you are. Know that your mother and I will be with you in spirit. Mr. Thompson will find a way to let us know how you're getting along." He held me close for a few seconds, then stepped back so Mom could give me a last hug. I felt her body tremble as I held her to me and kissed her cheek.

When Rob left me at the curb in front of Terminal B, I was troubled to see tears escape to his cheeks. I have never felt so close to him as when he held my hands and said, "I wish I could see you to the gate, but Washington has big eyes and even bigger ears. I'd better leave you here. You know I love you, Nonie, remember that. I'll be eagerly waiting to hear that you are settled. I hope you will be happy there, at least as happy as you can be under the circumstances." Suddenly he grabbed me in a bear hug then turned and hurriedly jumped in his car and sped away. I thought my heart would break.

At this point Daniel put the notebook down on the table beside his chair. "Whew," he let out a breath that he didn't know he had been holding in. Thinking aloud he muttered, "Rob, I guess that tells me something. Doc and Larry and all the rest are probably right. I shouldn't have let myself get so involved emotionally. But that's all right, as I told them, no matter what. I'm not a sniveling adolescent, for cripes sake."

He picked up the diary and started to read again. She wrote:

The trip from Dulles Airport to Seattle was uneventful; I noticed no strange looks even though there were two passengers on my flight who know me very well, my disguise is working. Immediately after landing I picked up my bags and hurried outside to hail a cab. It took only a few minutes to travel the few blocks to this gorgeous old historic inn bed and breakfast where I'll stay until tomorrow noon. I will spend the night in this beautiful room enjoying the view of the many ships anchored in the harbor. Puget Sound is located in the Salish Sea, an inland waterway that is part of the famed Inside Passage to Alaska. In reading Friday's brochure, I find that it was explored and charted most notably by Captain George Vancouver in 1792. Tomorrow I will travel to one of the more remote islands in the San Juans. These are the last hours of luxury I will know for some time to come. So beautiful here, Mt. Rainier in the distance, partly hidden by clouds.

April 3
Dear Diary,
Today is the day I go to my new home on Decatur Island. This morning I stumbled, sleepy eyed, into this lavishly appointed bathroom here in Friday's Inn, and was startled to see a strange woman looking back at me in the gold framed mirror. Oh no, that's me; that woman with the black, straight hair pulled back in a ponytail. I didn't expect to have such a drastic reaction to my new look. I turned on the water to wash my face, subconsciously, I think, feeling I could wash that stranger down the drain. I must, and I will, get accustomed to the look. The large horned-rim glasses erase any resemblance to my former self. I hurriedly dressed for my departure to the small island that I will call home for the foreseeable future.

I took the elevator down to the dining room. The service was great. My sausage omelet was good and the coffee divine. I must go there again before long.

After I finished breakfast I returned to my room, called a bellman to pick up my bag and made my way down to the landing. I shivered as a strong cool morning breeze chilled my body while I sat on a bench waiting for the small mail boat that would take me to the island where I will make my home for a while. I felt lonely as I waited to depart the San Juan Island Ferry Landing in Friday Harbor. I miss Mom and Dad and Rob.

April 4
Dear Diary,

About 3 o'clock yesterday afternoon I stepped out of the boat onto a small landing on Decatur Island. Mr. Smith, a school trustee, met the boat and took me to see the quaint little one-room school where I will teach the few children who live here in this beautiful, heavenly place. The school building is painted barn red; I suppose as protection against the elements, the humidity here is quite dense. The trim is creamy white, actually very attractive. I'm so lucky Mr. Thompson was able to obtain this position for me. He said there would be no more than eight or ten children attending the K through seventh grade taught here; once they start high school they take the family boat over to Lopez High School located on Lopez Island, seven miles to the west side of Decatur Island. I should be able to do a good job with the children here and still have time to work on the book I hope to write. My major in elementary education with a minor in journalism is perfect for my situation here; fate must have taken a hand. It's no longer safe for me to submit freelance articles to magazines or newspapers; perfect time to write the novel I've always wanted to write.

I was surprised when Mr. Smith informed me that only 190 or 200 people live full-time on this remote little island. It is accessible only by private boat or small plane. Just the kind of place I need to feel secure, something I have not felt these past few weeks in Washington, D.C. It's like a cocoon; this little cottage seems to enfold me in its arms. I have fallen in love with the place already. I feel at home in this small house the school is providing for me. Outside my window I see a green pacific tree frog sitting on madrona tree bark.

The little red schoolhouse and the boat dock are two of the most important features on the island; the school is the social heart of all activity.

The salary the school pays is minimal, but the school supplies, this house and everything in it is furnished. The Swedish modern furnishings are modest, but comfortable; the décor in rich colors of sienna and palm green are pleasing to the eye. I look forward to exploring the island before I have to get the school ready for the children.

COME SEPTEMBER

April 5
Dear Diary,
Four whole months to explore and perhaps visit some of the nearby islands, maybe go to Bellingham or Seattle to do a little shopping. Come September I'll be busy with my teaching duties. I'm grateful that Mr. Smith stocked the pantry with a few groceries before my arrival. I was happy to see the milk, orange juice, eggs, bread, and butter in the frig. The coffee was a welcome sight this morning. This afternoon I'll go to the small store I saw on my way here yesterday to stock up on a few essentials. Come September I'll be ready to start school; I look forward to teaching the children on this island. Come September, now that I think about it that's a good title for my novel. I hope to have it in stores by one year from this coming September.

April 6
Dear Diary,
If my book is in finished by June of next year as I plan, I will start book signings in some place far removed from Washington, D.C., in a place where I will not be recognized. The woman with the black hair pulled straight back in a pony tail with large horned-rimed glasses looking back at me from the small mirror over my sink resembles me in no way. I could fool my mother. That's good. My brown hair flowing to my shoulders, and my unfettered green eyes are things of the past, at least for a while to come. Rob almost fell over laughing when he saw me the morning I left Washington.

I went to the small general store today. I found most of the things I need, all the items necessary to keep the wolf from my door. It's surprising that the little store can provide so much, considering that everything has to be brought in by boat. Miss Pearl, as the locals call her, is the store owner as well as the postmistress. She is a wealth of information. Mail is brought in daily by a small plane. The first thing one sees upon landing is a grassy airstrip, and the waiting room for the air service. The small building that houses the store and the post office is just a block away. Everyone must pick up his or her mail from an assigned slot. I hope Miss Pearl doesn't think it strange that I receive mail from only one person. I'll have to order some magazines; that should help.

Miss Pearl tells me that all the children here like island life. She cites the freedom to play, horseback riding, the abundance of wildlife and lack of traffic noise. "There are cars but residents drive slowly on the dirt roads," she said. I personally am enamored of the wildflowers. Everywhere I look I see an abundance of color: violet, yellow, red and even blue.

April 7
Dear Diary,
I awoke this morning to the delightful chattering of small animals and the chirping of birds just outside my window; so different from the sounds of traffic I awakened to in my Washington, D.C., apartment. I felt wonderful, stretching and breathing in the fresh air. I'm still counting my blessings that Mr. Thompson was able to find this place for me. This afternoon I went for a walk in the woods. It was a short walk; I feared to venture out far alone, not being familiar with the island. The vegetation on this island is something like I have never seen. Large thigh-high ferns and plants that I don't recognize are growing under Sitka spruce. The perfume of the blossoms is heavenly. No doubt there is much to see and learn about this island. I headed back the way I came when a dense fog began to roll in; it was like a gray gauze blanket surrounding me. It felt a little eerie; I was concerned that I might lose my way. The cool, gossamer mist settled on my face and arms giving me a fresh, alive feeling. I walked back to the store filled with a feeling of confidence that I can face whatever challenge lies ahead of me and loving this island for it's beauty and the protection it affords me.

Most of the homes I saw on my walk are small cottages similar to the one I live in. All are well kept; beautiful rhododendrons gracing almost every yard, glorious colors of rose and white blossoms mixed with masses of shiny green foliage; the leaves look like someone polished them with wax.

When I arrived back at the store, I asked Miss Pearl for a suggestion for someone familiar with the island, someone I could ask to accompany me on my next outing. She said she was sure one of the girls here on the island would be happy to go with me. She jotted down a name and number on a slip of paper and handed it to me. "The one I would suggest is a real nature lover; she spends a lot of time in the woods learning about the flora and fauna of the island. Her name is Marjorie Anne Emerson. During the school year she is in Seattle pursuing a course of study that will enable her to create a naturalist center here when she graduates from the university."

"She sounds like just the person I need and would enjoy knowing. Thank you so much, Miss Pearl. I'll call her when I get settled in."

April 8
Dear Diary,
As I walked to the store today I saw a nice looking man leaving; he was headed for the dock. I ask Miss Pearl who he was. She said she didn't know his name; he just came in on the mail boat this afternoon. She laughed and said he was a curious one, "like all tourists, asking a lot of questions about the islands in the San Juans." Now that makes me a little jittery.

Most of the day spent at my computer creating an outline for *Come September*. In the evening I had a great dinner of Alaskan salmon, baked potato and salad. Read three chapters of the recently released *John Adams* by David McCullough. Interesting reading. One of the many books I brought with me. Off to bed.

At this point Daniel stretched and yawned; it had been a long busy day. He went downstairs, looked in the refrigerator, took out a cola drink and removed the cap. *This should keep me going for a while.*

April 9
Dear Diary,
This day was very much like the last: writing, reading, dinner, off to bed.

I find there are no air conditioners on the island. The overhead fans are adequate in this temperate climate. I wonder if one tires of the almost constant dampness. As for myself, I think the majestic scarlet sunsets make up for any small discomfort due to the fog and dampness.

When I sit on my little deck I can see goldfinch and many other species of birds flitting from limb to limb among the madrona trees.

April 10
Dear Diary,
Today I spoke with Miss Pearl again. She told me the best way to get to San Juan or the mainland is to reserve a seat on the mail plane. "Of course you have to be willing to make stops at the other small islands on the mail route." She stressed, "And be sure you can reserve a seat for your return trip."

I assured her, "Stopping at the other islands sounds good to me; it will help me get my bearing in this vast watery paradise."

Miss Pearl said, "Then there is always the small boat one can take to San Juan and from there on a larger boat to the mainland." I was happy to have this bit of information. I would still like to make at least one trip to Seattle and perhaps to Bellingham before school starts in the fall. I want to pick up some supplies for the school, items for decorating for holidays and items not available on the island.

Returning home I called Marjorie Anne. She sounded very friendly and I am to meet her tomorrow morning at 9 o'clock at the store to go exploring.

April 11
Dear Diary,
Trying to act nonchalant, I casually ask Miss Pearl if the stranger from yesterday had been in again. "Not a sign of him. I got the impression he is just one of those nosy tourist, seeing all he can cram in the few days he has left before leaving for wherever he lives."

Dear Lord I hope that is true.

Well, Dear Diary, I found a friend today. Marjorie Anne is a very interesting individual. She is eager to have someone go with her on her nature walks, a companion in her search of knowledge of all plants, animals, and even insects that inhabit this island. Raised on the island, she has two reasons for wanting to establish a nature center here. "It will attract tourists to the island," she said. "That will do wonders for the locals, bringing in badly needed income for the citizens and will help civic endeavors as well. Maybe some of the visitors will decide to stay, make their home here." Too, she is interested in all nature and wants to make it her life work. She is a likeable, intelligent girl. I'm looking forward to a pleasant association with her.

COME SEPTEMBER

Our walk was pleasant as well as informative. I found that many interesting animals inhabit this heavenly island; we saw deer, sheep, raccoons, muskrats, eagles, and snow owls. Offshore we saw seals and whales frolicking in the blue waters. The animals seem to know and love Marjorie Anne; some of the ones that skittered away from me yesterday came to her today and ate out of her hand.

April 12
Dear Diary,
I got my computer hooked up today. I am now ready to start to work on my novel. I have decided the names for some of my characters. My male protagonist in the story will be Darden, my female Madeline. Darden is a private eye, and Madeline is his sidekick. My title, *Come September* is to be a mystery with a romance thrown in. We'll see where it goes from here. I think I'll leave it up to my main characters, the two of them will show me which direction they want to go.

April 13
Dear Diary,
I manage to keep quite busy. I spend some time writing every day and some time working on lesson plans for the seven grades I'll be teaching. Seven grades in one room will be quite a challenge, but I can manage it. With so few children it shouldn't be too difficult.

Daniel read on through the diary, most of it about lesson plans, working on her novel and walking trips with Marjorie Anne in the forest. She described the climate, the plant life and animals they encountered. She also told about a trip she took into Seattle to buy supplies, take in a movie and do some shopping. While there they, again, visited an area called Old Town.
He read on—

April 13
Dear Diary,
On our walk today Marjorie Anne and I came upon a white iron bench settled under the shade of a tall madrona tree. We sat for a while talking about her hopes for a nature center for the island. She envisions students from other islands in the Sound and even from the

mainland, coming here to learn about their environment.

May 15
Dear Diary,
Marjorie Anne and sat I in deck chairs on the deck of the ferry we took to San Juan. We saw many lighthouses as we made our way through the small islands. The sky was awash with light purplish blue clouds.
Walking along South Beach we saw beautiful rock formations and crystal clear water. A lighthouse loomed large atop a mountain at Cattle Point. As we explored we came upon an old white building set in a grove of large cedar trees. Marjorie Anne told me it was once a British camp.
After a day of shopping and sightseeing and having a delightful tea at Fridays we reluctantly made our way back to the ferry landing. There we saw harbor seals basking on whale shaped rocks. A delightful day.

June 30
Dear Diary,
Sorry, Dear Diary, been too busy to visit you lately. Been busy exploring the island with Marjorie Anne. The two of us have also visited San Juan and some of the other islands as well as shopping in Billingham and Seattle.

July 4
Dear Diary,
What a day of celebration. I believe everyone on the island gathered at the little schoolhouse for a picnic; the fried chicken, potato salad and slaw tasted sensational, the best I ever ate. Then the ladies put a custard made of cream, sugar, eggs and vanilla in ice cream freezers, around which the men packed with ice and salt; the children sat on top of the freezers while the men turned the crank. Uhm, sensational. When dark settled on the island the men set off fireworks. Beautiful.

August 1
Dear Diary,
Been busy, busy working on my novel from morning to night. School starts soon and must ready schoolroom and finish lesson plans. Won't be seeing you for a while.

August 30
Dear Diary,
One more excursion into Seattle. While visiting there today Marjorie Anne and I toured Old Town again. First we relaxed in Doc Maynard's, a restored 1890s public house, pub and nightclub, where we heard the first part of the tour. From there, our guide led us along the sidewalks of Pioneer Square and into the areas below, which have been vacant since 1907.

We learned something of Seattle's history. It is a spooky city that lies underneath some of Seattle's present streets. I looked up through gratings and could see people walking on the streets above. It is a part of Seattle's very colorful past. One British gentleman on the tour told me about how his father was shanghaied from a pub in that subterranean city; it happened around 1904 when his father was only sixteen years old. He was given enough hard liquor to addle his brain, then thrown on a Chinese ship and taken out to sea where he was made to labor for eighteen months, no pay. Finally when the ship returned to Seattle he managed to escape.

Skipping ahead, Daniel came to the last entry. It was dated two days before he found her on the street in front of the bookstore.

October 18
Dear Diary,
This may be the most important entry in this journal. It includes a letter; I'm sending a copy of it to Mr. Thompson with a copy for him to give my father. Mr. Thompson doesn't want me to correspond directly with my folks, too much chance for mail tampering, might blow my cover. I'm instructing that this letter be opened only if I should disappear or meet an unexplained death.

Dear Mr. Thompson,

As you know my trouble started a few months ago when I interviewed a madam called Tillie. My purpose for the interview was to get information for an article that I intended to write about the seamy life of prostitution in the nation's capital. I wanted to explore what the life of a prostitute is like; where they are from, how and why they got into the business, what the life expectancy for them is in the business, and such as that.

Some of the people involved, mostly big names in Washington, apparently thought I would be naming names in the article. Not true. Tillie didn't give names in the interviews. She did mention that her clients came from all departments of the government including the Congress, the Senate, and the FBI, as well as other elite members of the Washington community. She gave me this information with explicit instructions not to use it. "If you do I'll deny that I ever met or heard of you. Your reputation as a reporter will be ruined," she said. Knowing that to be true, and due to the honor taught to me by my parents, I didn't intend to divulge that part of the interview. Someone must have thought I would; I started getting strange, nasty, phone calls. At first I thought little about it, but as time went on and the threats continued I became frightened.

Before I finished the article, Tillie was arrested and accused of espionage; they claimed she was passing classified information to Soviet Agents. The FBI claimed to have found that the Russians had established some of the girls in Tillie's place for the purpose of gathering information from her and the highly paid prostitutes with whom she worked; they also thought that some of the FBI agents might experience a slip of the tongue. I'm convinced that Tillie and most of the women were unaware that some of the women were connected in any way to the Russians.

The first night after her arrest, before lawyers could take a deposition from her, Tillie mysteriously died of a reported heart attack in her jail cell. Her medical records showed no history of heart trouble. Upon hearing of her death on the morning news, my father became frightened for my life. He called our attorney and friend, Mr. Edgar Thompson. "I fear for my daughter's life," my father told him. "How the hell can I protect her? I can't believe it is a coincidence that that Tillie person died a natural death her first night in jail." I admit Ed, that unbeknown to my father; I was listening on another line. I too became very frightened.

"Take it easy, Fred," you'll recall saying. "Come down to my office. We'll think of something." It was immediately announced that I would be traveling Europe and Asia for the foreseeable future. The news release stated that I would be doing a travel book, the subject being the most favorable locations of student hostels; best for safety and pleasure as well as education; the announcement was made hoping to keep those who would do me harm busy chasing shadows. Thank God, so far the ruse seems to be working. I live a fairly normal life, in my disguise, feeling somewhat secure and happy here on this lovely island. Thank you, Ed. It is my fervent hope that you never see this letter. I remain forever your grateful friend.

Sincerely,
Nonie Lee Talbert

When Daniel finished this entry in the diary he had an ah-ha moment. He surmised that the reason for Trudy's concern about the FBI finding out her whereabouts was since FBI agents, as well as other Washington movers and shakers, frequented Tillie's place, they might do her harm to keep their involvement from being made public; she thinks, and perhaps rightly so, that it is imperative to them now that they silence her, the connection has been made between Tillie's place and the Russians. It could easily become a national issue; heads could roll.

That does it, Daniel thought, *I've read enough*. He snapped the book shut. Rushing to the phone, he tripped over Tiger. "Ho, boy, move your big bod out of the way." He quickly dialed Lieutenant Mackey's number. "Sorry to call you at home so late again, Mackey, but we do have a dangerous situation on our hands. Trudy's fears of the FBI, or other D.C. big shots, are well founded, very real."

"That's hard to believe, Dan. What do you mean? Sure you are not just getting paranoid about the whole thing?"

"I am not; you'll agree with me when I tell you what I have to tell you. I just found something about Trudy's case I think you should know, and believe me when I say we are up against a real threat here. Can you spare some time to meet with me first thing in the morning?"

"Of course. What's up?"

"I'd rather sit down with you and discuss it in person if you don't mind. We need to work out a different plan to protect Trudy."

"Suits me. What about nine o'clock in the morning, my office?"

"Fine, I'll see you there."

He quickly dialed Cynthia's number. "Sorry to call so late, but I need you to open the store for me in the morning. Can you do it?"

"Yes, but..."

"Great." Daniel hastily hung up the phone, not giving Cynthia time to ask questions.

I've read all I need to read of Trudy's diary for now. I'll hide it here in the bookshelf. He placed the notebook on its side in the middle of the shelf and stacked *Encyclopedia Britannica* in front of it. He took particular pains to see that the outside door was securely locked. *That should keep it safe for a while,* he thought.

"Come, Tiger. Let's take our walk." Tiger yelped. "Wups, sorry I stepped on your foot, ol' fellow." Tiger wagged his bushy tail and ran to the door. He followed Daniel downstairs and waited impatiently while his master opened the closet door and took his leash from a hook and clipped it to his collar.

While walking through the neighborhood, Daniel felt that watchful eyes were following him. Again he thought, *My imagination might be getting the best of me. Still, for Mom's safety I will ask Lieutenant Mackey to put an officer on guard at the house.* After a brisk walk he turned and walked up the driveway, taking the outside stairs to the door to his apartment in the back part of the house.

He showered, brushed his teeth, and went to bed. It was late; he was bone tired. Shortly after he fell asleep a low, guttural sound, then loud barking awakened him. When suddenly Tiger sprang at the open window, scratching at the screen, he realized the sound came from the dog's throat. He jumped up, ran to the door and opened it. Looking up and down the driveway he saw a shadow just before it disappeared around the corner at the back of the house. *I could call the police but I don't think they are in for chasing shadows,* he reasoned. *I'll inform Mackey in the morning.*

Chapter 8

Daniel awoke later than usual, conscious that Tiger was licking his hand in anticipation of his morning outing. *I must be more exhausted than I realized.* He rubbed his eyes, headed for the bathroom and splashed water on his face. "Okay, okay, Tiger. I know it's time for your walk. Maybe a good run will clear the fog from my brain." He went quietly down to the kitchen, put coffee on to brew, poured a glass of juice, and heated a muffin in the microwave. He hurriedly finished his breakfast, propped a note to his mother against the sugar bowl suggesting that she keep Tiger in the house with her today, hinting that the dog might be sick and he didn't want him out in the heat.

He set off for his appointment with Lieutenant Mackey. He was stopped while rushing past the receptionist's desk. "Wait, mister, you have to sign in; I'll see if the lieutenant can see you."

"It's okay, I have an appointment with him at nine o'clock." Not stopping to get her permission he hurried past her, opened the door and said to the lieutenant, "We have a bigger problem than we realized, Mackey."

"Hold on, I'm not the enemy here. Slow down and tell me what happened."

"There are FBI, Russian spies, and Washington big shots involved in this thing. It's no damn wonder that Trudy is scared half out of her wits." He told him what he found in the diary. "What do you think we should do, Mackey?"

"We, we, Dan? We should do nothing. I will take care of it. Where did you get all this information?"

At first Daniel avoided the question. "Believe me it comes from a good source. Aw, hell, I may as well tell you; you have to know sooner or later. I read Trudy's diary."

"If it wouldn't be too presumptuous of me to ask, it might be helpful for me to know..." he hesitated, tight-lipped, "where the hell did you get that diary?"

"It was in a false bottom in her briefcase."

"We found the false bottom, there was nothing there."

"I looked there before you did."

"You took the diary out before returning the briefcase to me? You do know that is tampering with evidence, don't you?"

Daniel felt like he was tripping over his tongue. "Well, yes I did, but I gave Trudy my word before she gave me permission to hand the case back to you."

"We didn't need her permission to retain the item in question for evidence. I was trying to be kind to a damsel in distress when I let her keep it for a while. I don't appreciate your deviousness, Dan."

"I know, Lieutenant. I hoped you'd understand after you see what her diary contains; after you see why she doesn't know in whom she can trust. She is really frightened, and with good cause."

By now the lieutenant was losing patience with Daniel's meddling. "I see. Spill it, Dan, and it better be good. You know I could have you brought up on charges for withholding evidence. That diary should have been turned over to the police immediately after you found out about it. I don't know if I can protect you on this one, Dan. I'd advise you to stop playing do-gooder, savior, detective, whatever it is you think you are doing. If you don't, I'd advise you to get a good lawyer, you're going to need one. I can't afford to hang my hide out to dry just so you can play cops and robbers, and Mr. Good Guy."

"I know, but Trudy is afraid of the FBI. She didn't want you to see the diary before I read it so I could explain to you why it is important that the FBI not be called in on this. I intended all along to give it to you after I read it and got Trudy's permission to do so."

"So you and this Trudy feel that I wouldn't be bright enough to figure out why she is so frightened if you didn't read the diary first and explain it to the dumb cop? Come on, Dan. Give me a little credit. All that business about not letting the FBI know where she is, I can tell you that's an exercise in futility. The FBI picked up her trail the day before she left the island, but since they didn't have her under surveillance the morning she got hit, they couldn't be sure who the perpetrator was, or so they say. He got away."

"You mean they knew where she was all the time and you didn't tell me?"

"You don't think I tell you everything I find out, do you? I have enough trouble keeping you halfway under control as it is. And yes, they did pick up her trail, but they kept bungling the job, not finding what they needed to know about who was interested in the information in the briefcase. They picked up her tail again the week after she was attacked. Actually, they say they knew her life would be in danger if the Russian spies found out where she was. At least that is what they want us to believe. My theory is that they hoped the spies would find her enabling them to catch them and, of course, protect what they thought might be their star witness at the same time. They had no way of knowing that she didn't know who the players were. They suspect that one of their own is feeding information to the Russians. If they have a rogue agent in their midst, they want to find out who it is and take appropriate action. The Russians didn't know they were suspect; at least that is what the FBI thinks, or wants to think. The Feds think the Russians are responsible for Tillie's death, and they think that as far as the Russians know, the FBI thinks Tillie's death was an accident caused by a fall on the concrete floor splitting her head open; all the while telling the media that she died of a heart attack. I guess they thought accident might sound suspicious. Heart attacks do happen in jail many times; a person can't take the strain of being caught doing whatever they were arrested for and being thrown in jail with a bunch of wild-eyed petty crooks, dopers, even murderers. It gets to them. It can be very stressful; therefore a heart attack."

"I'm puzzled about this Russians spy thing. The cold war is over."

"My man, they still have spies in this country, and we have spies in theirs."

"So the spies got away?"

"I don't think so; the news out of Washington this morning sounds like they think they got their man or men as the case may be; naturally they don't mention the Tillie case, just that they have in custody a suspected Russian spy. The mystery is, do they have him and if so, how come it took them so long."

"Who was the mugger? FBI, Russian agent, or some local two-bit scumbag?"

"It was a local scumbag, but who knows who paid him to do it. Some Washington big-wig or piece of human garbage right out of the FBI ranks, or it could be the Russians."

Daniel asked, "Which one do you think?"

"Listen, Dan, don't you ever get tired of badgering me to tell you something that I don't know, or if I did I couldn't tell you? Your meddling is getting a little wearisome. As you know, the briefcase had one fingerprint on it, and the handbag was found a couple of weeks ago in a trash heap near the Rio Grande. The thief didn't leave any money in it, but he left fingerprints galore inside. A savvy criminal would not have left fingerprints on the briefcase or handbag. When they apprehend him, and they will, they'll put the screws to him to divulge the name of the person who hired him. Only trouble there is he may not know; the culprit probably used an assumed name. Luckily Trudy Rose used travel checks made out in the name Trudy Morgan, her non-deplume, and cash; she had no credit cards with her because of the incognito thing. Of course, if she had credit cards, the thief probably couldn't resist the temptation to use them; that would make him easier to find, so now that I think about it, maybe it was unfortunate that she didn't use credit cards. They sent the mugger's fingerprints to Washington for analysis. He has been in trouble before and his identity was readily available. Looks like it will be a while before they find him. He left town; no trace of him has been found."

"I hope it won't be too long."

Lieutenant Mackey seemed to loosen up a bit. "You know, it's not unthinkable that some of the FBI men would frequent a house of prostitution, and it's not unthinkable that they might do away with a spy, or maybe even a madam whom they considered a threat to the country, maybe even to themselves, but what is unthinkable is that they would try to harm an American journalist. There must be an explanation for all of this."

Daniel was not convinced about the effectiveness of the investigation but knew he was in over his head. "I'll go by the hospital and tell Trudy that I must give the diary to you."

"You do that. And again Dan, make it clear to her that we don't have to have her permission. I can get an order for a search warrant if you and she persist in hiding evidence. Can you think of any reason for the FBI to go so far as to harm a journalist?"

Daniel was ready with an answer. He had had a long sleepless night to think about it. "Yes, I'd say there is an explanation; they may be perceived to have knowingly or unknowingly passed secret information to the enemy through the prostitutes. And too, there is the chance that some or all of them are married men. Neither their wives nor, I presume, their bosses would be pleased with such activity. And there is the matter of the courts to be reckoned with. There could be serious charges, perhaps as serious as treason. Any of these reasons could explain their willingness to take whatever measures possible to keep Tillie from testifying and Trudy from writing about it."

"I see your point, but I think you are wrong. I would rather think they are just trying to scare her into keeping quiet. However, I'll do all in my power to get to the bottom of it, and as always, I'll keep a twenty-four-hour watch on the so-called Miss Trudy Rose. But get that diary in my hands, the sooner the better."

"Thanks, Lieutenant. I have another favor to ask."

"Shoot."

"I'm worried about the safety of my mom. Someone was looking in my apartment window last night. Whoever it was disappeared around the corner before I got a good look at them. Might have been just a prowler, but all the same I would like police protection for Mom, especially when I can't be at home."

"You're asking a lot, Dan, but I'll see what the chief will do. Now, get that diary to me, pronto. Now, Dan, listen to me. You go home and get that diary and bring it back here to me. Don't let your coattail touch you twice until it is in my hands. Are you hearing me, Dan Lindsey?"

"Yes, sir," Daniel clicked his heels together and saluted.

"Don't be a smart ass, Dan. Get out of here and do what I told you to do. I'll have to try to save your blasted hide one more time."

"Sorry, Mackey."

Daniel didn't wait for his usual time in the afternoon to visit Trudy. He rushed from Lieutenant Mackey's office to the hospital. He found Trudy more alert than ever, but with alertness came heightened fear. The look in her eyes made it clear to Daniel that she was worried. "Why the frown, Trudy? Are you uncomfortable?"

"No, I'm frightened, Dan. I have a feeling someone is watching me. It was a mistake for me to leave the island; I know that now. I thought my disguise was complete, that no one would recognize me."

"Trudy Rose, try to relax. Lieutenant Mackey has someone watching your room twenty-four hours a day."

"I don't think so. The past day or two I have only occasionally seen a policeman in the hall outside my door."

"They aren't always in uniform, Trudy. Rest assured, they are here; that may be why you feel that someone is watching you. It's probably an officer in plain clothes."

"I hope so. Dan, what would I do without you? Nurse Abigail said you felt, at first, that my being hurt was somehow your fault. Lucky for me you thought that. What if it had happened somewhere else, down the street a ways? You probably would have read in the paper about a woman found mysteriously murdered, no suspect, like those young ladies that Nurse Abigail told me about being murdered in Juarez."

"But that didn't happen, and now you are safe." *God, let that be true.* "Trudy Rose, I have to turn the diary over to Lieutenant Mackey. I've known him and about his work as a detective for a long time; I trust him implicitly."

"And I trust you, Dan. Do what you have to do."

After reassuring her as best he could, he hurried off to collect the diary for Lieutenant Mackey. Upon arriving home, Daniel entered through the front door, and gave a low whistle. Tiger came bouncing from the family room nervously prancing around, wagging his tail speedier than usual, and ran upstairs ahead of Daniel. Upon entering his suite, Tiger started acting even more strange, running around sniffing, making a low growling sound. Looking around, Daniel noticed that the outside door leading to the balcony was ajar. It had been pried open. He saw nothing out of place. He quickly started pulling books from the shelf in front of where he had left the diary. It was not there. "Damn, stupid, stupid," he scowled aloud. "I should have left my door open so Tiger could have gotten in. Any fool would think to look there." He closed the door leaving Tiger inside, being careful to cover the knob with a handkerchief to avoid blurring any fingerprints that might be there. *Awe hell, any idiot would wear gloves to break and enter, especially the FBI.*

Since nothing else is disturbed, someone must have known where to look. But how? Daniel tried to think. He walked to the window and looked out at the steep pitched roof of the house next door. He slapped his forehead with the palm of his hand. I forgot about that house being empty. "Tiger, your master is a an absolute imbecile." Preparing himself for a barrage of heated words, he placed another call to Lieutenant Mackey. He minced no words, thinking it best to take whatever the lieutenant had to say and get it over with. "Me again Mackey. The diary is gone; someone jimmied the lock on my door."

He heard a loud sigh. "That is bad news. Dan, if I were a swearing man I would tell you what I'm really thinking right now."

"And I asked you to assign someone to watch my house for my mother's safety. If there had been a uniform around it wouldn't have happened."

"Don't try to turn this thing around, Dan. I told you, you should have given it to me for safekeeping. Tell me about it. Where did you keep it?"

"It was in my bookshelf, behind a set of encyclopedia Britannica. Nothing else in the room was disturbed. Someone had to know where it was."

"And who might that someone be? Have there been any strangers in the house?"

"No, not that I know of."

"How about your cleaning lady, your lawn man?"

"I trust our helpers; Carmen has been with us for years, and Peter even longer. The blame is all mine, Mackey. I don't always close my blinds. All the other houses on this block are one story including the one next door. No one can see in my upstairs window. It just dawned on me that the house next door is empty now. Someone with binoculars could have climbed onto the roof to see into my window. My bookshelves are across from the window. I have been very careful since I saw that light blue Taurus tailing me, but someone must have followed me home and seeing me with the diary in my hand, wanted to have a look-see at it, see what it was."

"Yeah, probably with binoculars, as you say."

"You know, I told you someone has been sneaking around the house. The person was most likely watching last night as I readied for bed; probably saw the light go on in my room, and saw me put the diary behind the books. What a numbskull I am to have been so careless with it. It should have been kept in a safety deposit box, away from the house."

"I have to agree with you about the numbskull part, but it should have been under lock and key in a filing cabinet here at police headquarters," Lieutenant Mackey stated emphatically.

"I know, I know. I feel terrible. In trying to protect Trudy, I've let her down."

"Don't be so hard on yourself, man. You can't think of everything. I don't know another soul who would be as diligent as you are at caring for a person they don't even know."

"I feel that I do know her now." *I still wonder who this Rob is.*

"Go easy, Dan. You don't really know anything but what you read in the diary. Diaries aren't always factual. You know this lady writes fiction."

"Since she has been here she has been in a coma, and when not in a coma she has been mostly incoherent; not able to fabricate a story. And some of what I'm basing my judgment on is what she has said, not altogether what is in the diary. She is just now beginning to think straight."

"You have something there. Sit tight. I'll get right on this latest screw up right away."

"Screw up is right," Daniel admitted.

Disheartened and disgusted with himself, Daniel went to the store to relieve Cynthia. She asked, "Did you have a problem this morning, Dan? You seemed quite upset when you called."

"Nothing special. I just wanted to talk to the lieutenant for a while," he answered. She seemed satisfied with that answer and left the store to go across the street for coffee and doughnuts. "Do you want glazed or cake?"

"Neither." He didn't feel like eating. "Just bring me coffee with cream."

After closing the store at 6 o'clock, Daniel stopped at El Muños for a snack. He made a special point to sit in Manuel's section. "Bring me a double scotch and soda, Manny. No, wait, better make it a single. I'll order food a little later." *The shape I'm in a double might impair my driving to say nothing of my senses which don't seem too sharp as it is.*

Manuel returned with Daniel's drink. "Oh, *Señior,* I'm glad to see you. That man you thought was following you came in earlier. He looked all around and left after he had only coffee. I gave him evil eye for you. That okay? *Sí?*"

"*Sí,* that's okay. Thanks, Manny. Bring me a fajita plate, please. He dipped tostados in hot tomatillo salsa and sipped his drink while he waited, all the time keeping a watchful eye, but saw nothing of the burly looking man he had encountered here and in the hospital parking lot a few days earlier. He bid goodnight to Manny and the cashier as he left the restaurant. *Now that they have the diary I guess they don't need to watch me anymore.*

Chapter 9

The next morning before heading for the store, Daniel took Tiger for a short walk. In the past he often took Tiger to the store and let him stay behind the counter. "I'm leaving you in charge, boy," he said to Tiger. *Closing the barn door after the cows are out,* he thought. "Not that you, you big excuse for a watchdog, would be much help. You stay downstairs with Mom today and keep the boogers away. Don't worry, I'll be back before your walk time."

He called down to his mother. "Let Tiger out for a few minutes around noon, will you, Mother? Otherwise keep him in the house; I don't want him to get heartworms." That was the best excuse he could come up with for keeping him inside. "I've given him breakfast and changed his water." The intruder had what he came for. He wasn't really concerned that he or she would return and harm his mother, but just to be safe he thought it best if Tiger remained inside.

"Why on earth are you in such a hurry? Tiger doesn't like to stay in the house. He just went on a barking spree yesterday, running up to your room and back down to the back door. He wanted to be outside."

"Mom, just please do that for me. I'll explain another time." *I won't tell her the real reason Tiger was running up to my room, no use worrying her.*

Daniel had a very difficult time trying to keep his mind on the business at hand that morning. He did the usual routine of opening the store, by rote. When he waited on customers, he made an effort to be polite and helpful, all the time wishing Cynthia would come in so he could leave. He wanted to see Trudy, but he would not tell her the diary was missing.

The loud ringing of the telephone caused him to jump. He picked it up on the first ring, and was relieved to hear Lieutenant Mackey's voice. "Good morning, Dan. We may have a bit of good news."

"We can use it, but what do you mean, may have?"

"Don't get too excited. It may be a hoax made by a crook, or it may be legitimate; on the other hand it may be just a crank wanting to make trouble or get attention. About an hour ago I had a phone call. A voice said, 'Listen and don't ask questions. You and that store owner can ease up. I'm not one of the bad guys; we have everything under control. The diary is safe in our hands. And please, tell that half-baked store owner playing detective to butt out. He is about to mess up our investigation.'"

The lieutenant spoke very emphatically. " So I'm giving you the message, Dan, butt out. I think it was a *bona fide* call from someone who is working on the case. He sounded sincere. A crook would not have bothered to call; they would be long gone with the evidence. I asked, 'Who are you? If you are FBI come in and make yourself known to me. We can work together on this?' 'I didn't say I was FBI,' he said. The phone clicked. The caller was gone. I do feel the call was legit."

"But what if it wasn't? Besides, it's the FBI Trudy is afraid of. He may have been trying to lull us into thinking Trudy is safe."

"Dan, if it was the FBI they have known all along where she is. I'll get back to you as soon as I know more. Now listen, Dan, I'm going to give it to you straight; we have done our best on this thing. We'll keep up the investigation, but I want your word that you will stand aside and let us handle it. If it was the FBI, and I think it was, he is right. You could screw up the works. The FBI will not feel free to give us information if they think you are privy to everything they tell me. I'll keep you posted as best I can. Now just try to relax and let us handle it. Will you?""

"Of course. I have no choice."

"Now you are getting the idea, buddy."

Chapter 10

Daniel didn't know what to make of it the following day as he walked down the hall on the fourth floor of the hospital, and turned to enter Trudy's room when a well-built, intelligent looking man stepped in front of him, just long enough to smile and wink. Then he stepped aside and with his left arm flung back toward the door, waved him into Trudy's room. Daniel thought, *What the hell?* But somehow the encounter left him feeling more confident that things would work out, that it was the FBI who had the diary, but was that good? He hoped so.

A smiling Trudy was sitting up in bed. She wore the pink quilted robe Cynthia had loaned her. Her hair had a half-inch of growth of light brown at the roots and was still black on the ends. It was tied back with a pink ribbon. "My, aren't we foxy today, Miss Trudy Rose." Daniel greeted her, kissed her cheek and handed her a dozen long stem yellow roses. "Yellow roses for the gal I found in Texas." He whistled a few bars of "Yellow Rose of Texas."

"Oh, so you are still giving me a middle name. I rather like it."

"It's just temporary, that is unless you'd like it to be permanent."

"I would, I'd like that; but only for you, no one else. You are a happy fellow today. Did you win the lottery?" She crooked her forefinger at him, motioning for him to come near. I'll tell you a secret." She whispered in his ear as he leaned close to her, "My real name is Nonie Lee Talbert. Promise you won't tell."

"Cross my heart." He was so glad to see her happy and playful. He didn't tell her she had already told him that her name was Nonie Lee and he had read Talbert in her diary.

The next few days piled one on the other with no word from Lieutenant Mackey. Nonie Lee, as Daniel now knew her to be, began to feel better and restless. He thought, *There is no need to keep calling her Trudy, the cat is out of the bag, but she likes Trudy Rose and I do too.*

He decided it was time to call Lieutenant Mackey. "Any word yet?"

"I can tell you this much. I believe the call the other day was legitimate, that it was from a law enforcement person who has Miss Morgan's best interest at heart. I believe we have nothing to fear from them, but there is still someone else out there that we must find and apprehend before we are out of the woods. Somebody had to hire the scumbag that mugged her."

"The large burly man?" asked Daniel.

"Don't jump to conclusions, Dan. The large burly man could be the FBI, a legitimate one. They've been watching you from the start, I believe, just waiting for you to find something that would be helpful to the investigation."

"Are you telling met me the FBI took the diary from my house?"

"I didn't say that."

"You didn't have to. You know my mother lives with me; or rather I live with her. For that reason alone, it's a relief to know, or at least to think, that it wasn't some bloodthirsty killer prowling around the place."

"Rest easy, my friend. It's in their hands now, and you and I must stand aside, stay out of their way. I hope they'll keep me informed."

From that conversation Daniel felt assured that it was the FBI that entered his house, and that they meant no harm to Trudy or something unpleasant would have already happened to her, something more than the lump on her head.

"But wait a minute, Mack. Rest easy? What about the snaky eyed bozo who has been following me around? He's probably the one who clubbed Trudy."

"I thought you said he was burly, you said nothing about snaky eyes."

"There have been both, a burly one and a snaky eyed one."

"I see. I don't know who that could be; it could be another FBI man. By the way, Dan, you can call her by her real name now, Nonie Lee Talbert. It's no longer a secret."

"How do you know her real name; I didn't tell you."

"We have our ways."

"I see," Daniel said, purposely mocking the lieutenant. "I think she likes me to call her Trudy Rose now. She is accustomed to it."

"So I've heard, but if you don't mind, I'd prefer to call her Miss Talbert now."

Chapter 11

"That burly, snaky eyed character could be one of the bad guys, Dan, but the FBI, as well as other agencies, employ snaky eyed characters, too. Not all of them look like Paul Newman, you know. And when I said rest easy, I meant just that. Rest easy. They have a handle on that too, I think."

"Yeah? I wonder. If those bozos who have been following me are FBI they need to sharpen their tailing skills."

"This town is rife with informants. One of them will come up with something."

Daniel answered, "Russian spies, if it is Russian spies, don't pal around in that circle. I doubt that they let slip secrets to informants."

"You'd be surprised with the type of misfits they hire when they need to get information from local riffraff. You know, fight fire with fire. And who is the expert that says a Russian spy is responsible for clubbing Trudy, er, er, Miss Talbert?"

"If not the FBI, who else?"

"Who knows? That's what we are working on finding out. The agent I'm dealing with tells me they have a lead on the FBI agent who is passing information to the Russians. All he will say about it is, 'Watch the papers, you'll see and hear plenty about it later on."

Daniel thought, *I have to be satisfied with that for now. But the way the FBI, if that's who it is, has been operating lately I wonder how well they are protecting Trudy. If they lost her trail after she left the island, they could do it again.* He stopped at the hospital on his way to the store. Rushing happily into Nonie Lee's room carrying a beaker of hot coffee for her and one for himself, he expected to have a pleasant conversation with her. He found there was no one guarding her door; it was closed. He knocked, when there was no answer he walked in calling, "Hey, sleeping beauty, it's time to rise and shine."

The bed was empty. He stood around a minute or two before he noticed that the bedside table held an open book, no other items. *Good sign, she's well enough to concentrate on reading.* He knocked on the bathroom door, no answer. He opened it, no one there. By this time he had the picture. They must have taken her for tests. He rushed to the nurses' station. "Where is Trudy? Is she undergoing more tests this morning?" The hospital staff was still not aware that her name was Nonie Lee Talbert.

"What do you mean? She's in her room as far as I know."

"As far as you know? I just came from there and she is not there."

"Maybe she is in the bathroom."

"I'm telling you she is not there."

Nurse Abigail rushed to Nonie Lee's room. She checked the bathroom and closet. Convinced at last that she was not in her room, she ran into the hall calling out, "Patient missing, 447." Orderlies came running, going into every room, then some went to the basement, some to the other floors.

When they exhausted all hopes of finding her, Daniel yelled aloud, "Damn, they've kidnapped her. Damn the FBI. Damn Mackey, with his placating." He didn't care who heard him. He ran to the elevator, and when he saw that it was stopped on the twelfth floor he started running down the hall to the stairwell. He took the four flights, two steps at a time. He blinked his eyes as he stumbled onto the sun-bright parking lot, jumped into his car, and headed for police headquarters.

When Daniel entered, Lieutenant Mackey's office, he found him with his feet propped up on his desk, reading the morning paper. He was furious. *There he sits, reading the damn paper.* He blurted out, "Nonie Lee is missing; I suppose you're going to tell me the FBI has her safe under surveillance. I just came from the hospital. She is not in her room. Nobody knows where she is."

"Let's think about it. You know the FBI doesn't go around telling their business to everybody. I don't know if they have her or not."

"What the hell, Mackey? Did you know they've got Nonie Lee? Just sit there and read your paper; do you care that she is missing?"

"Well, good morning to you, too, Mr. Lindsey. Take it easy. Have a seat before you fall on your behind."

The dingy buff colored walls seemed to be whirling around. Daniel plopped in the chair on the opposite side of the desk from Lieutenant Mackey. "I'm waiting for an answer to my question."

"Which one?"

"Did you know she is missing?"

"I wondered how long it would take you to discover that Miss Talbert is not in her hospital room."

"Where is she? I want to see her."

"I can't tell you that."

Daniel got up from his chair and leaned across the desk. "Do you mean to tell me that you don't know where she is, and you're telling me to take it easy? To hell with all of you, I'll find her." He turned and started to the door.

"Come back here, Dan. Now sit down and shut up before I have you arrested for disorderly conduct. I did know she was missing. I'm waiting now for word from the captain about what can be done."

"How would you know? The hospital staff didn't know until I found out and raised hell with them."

"I feel sure she's safe. Believe me, brother, I know how you feel, but until we are sure who all the players are in this game, they may be keeping her out of sight. Leave it alone; the less said about it the better. Surely you can understand that."

Lieutenant Mackey thought, *I hate to tell this hotheaded man that I don't know where his imagined ladylove is; he will go off the deep end.*

"All right. You made your point." He started to walk away.

"Wait, Dan. Now settle down and believe me when I tell you all of this is coming together. You wouldn't want to jeopardize the case by the wrong person or persons finding out where she is. When I tell you I can't tell you where she is, I mean just that because I don't know."

"I suppose the FBI is holding her for interrogation," Daniel grumbled.

"I expect the persons in charge do have some questions for her, but the main reason for hiding her, if they are hiding her, is to keep her safe until they are sure about what is going on. Go on to your store and keep busy until further notice."

"The store? Oh hell, it's after opening time. I forgot about it."

"See what I mean? Concentrate on your business and let us take care of our business. Trust me on this, Dan. I do know the authorities know she is not in her room; I just don't know how and what they know, just that I was told to keep a lid on it when you, Dan, find out she's gone. I think that means they know what is going on."

Daniel shook his head and turned to leave.

"Take it easy," Lieutenant Mackey called after him as he walked out the door.

Take it easy he says. Easy to say, hard to do, Daniel thought. He arrived at the store to find two customers entertaining themselves by looking in the window while waiting for the door to open. "Sorry folks, running a little late this morning." He unlocked the door and stood back to let the ladies enter. Immediately he saw large boxes of books he had brought from the storeroom the night before but had not shelved. *Mackey is right. I need to concentrate on the store. I've been letting things slip lately.*

Chapter 12

Early the morning of Nonie Lee's disappearance from the hospital a man whom she had not seen before entered her room. He was of sturdy build, some might even say rotund. A black knit cap covered his hair, and his eyes were covered with dark sunglasses. He wore a black leather jacket over rumpled khaki pants. "Miss Talbert, I've been instructed to take you for an MRI. Please put on your robe and house slippers."

Oh me gosh, he knows my real name. "Who are you?"

"I'm your guard for the day, working undercover, name's Jim Parker."

"They usually send an orderly for me."

"I know. It's tough all over. Not enough help today. Make haste, honey."

She didn't like the way he said 'honey'; rather sarcastic, she thought. She stood on wobbly legs, reached to the foot of her bed, and picked up her robe, put it on and slipped her feet into her slippers and said, "Let me wash my face and run a comb through my hair."

"Don't bother. They are waiting for you in radiology."

"Radiology? What for? An MRI you said? I don't think so, I'm not due for tests today."

"Listen, lady, I'm not paid to answer questions." With that he took her arm and led her to an empty elevator. She noticed the door was propped open. She gave him a quizzical look. He put his hand on her back and gave her a little nudge. He pushed the down button. On the first floor, the elevator door opened. He thrust out his arm for her to take. When she failed to take it, he took a firm hold on her arm and propelled her down the hall toward an outside door.

"Jim, if that is what you say your name is, radiology is in the basement."

"Please be quiet; don't make a fuss. You are goin' to like this ride."

He is not a guard; I think he is lying. She pulled away from him with all her strength, but in her weakened condition she was helpless to break free. She tried to scream; he clamped his hand tight over her mouth and rushed her out a side door. A car was waiting. In it sat a woman dressed in what looked to

Nonie Lee like a waitress or nurse uniform; a big pink organza handkerchief flowed from a breast pocket. The woman got out and opened the back door, helped the man push Nonie Lee into the car, slid in beside her and quickly closed the door. Jim jumped in behind the wheel and drove out of the parking lot. All the time Nonie Lee was trying to scream, but no sound escaped, even her voice had become weak with her illness.

"Don't bother trying to holler, lady; no one will hear you; not even the birds are out this early."

Finally her voice came out in a hoarse whisper, "Where are you taking me and why?"

The woman chewed gum furiously. "My name is Veda, honey." She put her arm around Nonie's shoulder. "You have nothing to fear, we are taking you to a safe place. We would have come for you sooner, but we had to wait until you were able to eat and drink, in other words we waited for you to get off the feeding tube."

The man spoke crossly, "Put a lid on it, Veda. That's enough."

Veda gave her shoulder a little squeeze. "Just keep quiet dearie, you'll be all right."

Jim spoke up. "Quit yer bitchin', lady. We feel it's time to get you out of there. Let you get a little fresh air, go for a ride. I'd think you'd like that."

Nonie Lee didn't like the sound of that. *Go for a ride sounds like a one-way trip, like the way they used it in the gangster movies.* She thought it unlikely that she would like it. *They're getting me out of there so they can try to make me talk or to keep me from telling what I know, or what they think I know.* "I knew you were not my guard."

"Sure, lady. Sure."

What happened to my guard? You're not taking me to a safe place. I was in a safe place."

"Safe place in there? Yeah, is that why I could just walk in and take you out of there, no questions asked."

"I want to know what happened to my guard."

"Officers have to go to the men's room occasionally, and lady cops have to visit the powder room, you know. Now just settle down and behave yourself; much better for you and better for my nerves. You don't want to make me nervous, now do you? When I get nervous, it's not a pretty sight."

They drove for hours through mountains, and then along a river. They stopped a couple of times for a restroom break. Veda stayed in the car with Nonie Lee while Jim went in for a few minutes, then Veda took her in with her.

They stopped to pick up take-out food twice along the way. Nonie Lee saw a city limit sign that read, "Marathon population 455." Again, Veda stayed in the car with her while Jim went in for sandwiches and drinks. Weary and weak, Nonie Lee had no appetite; she fell asleep. When she awoke, they were on a small highway, headed south. Soon she discovered that they were taking her into a sleazy motel room. "Where are we? Where have you taken me?"

"All you need to know is that you are here with Veda and me." Aside to Veda he said, "We better placate her, can't have her making a fuss, screaming and yelling, causing the help to call in the local police. These small-town ignoramuses would like nothing better than to get in on something like this and become overnight heroes."

About this time in Washington, D.C., a middle-aged couple was getting ready for early evening snack of cheese, crackers and fruit. They had no appetite for a full meal. He said, "Come on, dear, eat something; have a glass of sherry. You know you told Rob you would try to relax. You are looking thinner than you have since you were a girl. Have you weighed yourself lately?"

"I haven't; my weight is the least of my worries. I know something has happened to her, otherwise she would have found a way to contact us, or at least she would have been in touch with Ed, and I am trying to relax, it's impossible. When you pour my sherry you better have one yourself. You aren't exactly Mr. Calm."

"I need something stronger than sherry. I may just have a double scotch."

"Ed says he doesn't think there is anything to worry about. He thinks she is just being cautious, being smart; she doesn't want them to be able to trace her. She is busy promoting her book." He didn't really believe what he was saying, but trying as best he could to keep his wife from being upset.

"All the same, I want Rob to see what he can find out, start phoning around the places where she is most likely to be or to have gone. He could even go to those towns and ask questions, take a picture of her, find out if any one has seen her."

"That would defeat the purpose of her going into hiding. We don't want that, do we?"

"Well no, but I don't know how much longer I can carry on as if nothing has happened, smiling and saying she is having a wonderful time in her travels around Europe, knowing all the time she may have come to harm."

"I know, dearest, but let's just wait a little longer before we panic and do something that would perhaps expose her agenda."

Meanwhile in that small South Texas town, Jim could see Nonie Lee was alarmed. "It's all right, lady. You'll be fine. We'll have a little talk after Veda gets back with something to eat. I hope you can eat a bowl of soup and drink a milkshake. Shake a leg, Veda. I'm hungry."

All at once she felt hungry, hungrier than she had been since she left the island. "I would rather have a hamburger and french fries."

"I said soup and milkshake today. I don't want to feed you something that is too harsh for you, make you sick, don't want you puking all over the place. Got that, Veda? Soup and milkshake for the lady." Veda heard these remarks as she put on her sunglasses and hat. Opening the door she faced the hot, bright south Texas sun.

Later Veda appeared with the food. "What a line I had to go through to get this food. I've stood until my feet are aching."

"You were gone long enough, did they have to butcher the cow and grind the meat for the hamburgers?"

"Very funny," Veda snapped. "If you think you can do better you can go next time." She took off her sunglasses, slung them on the bed and plopped down in the chair next to Nonie Lee.

Jim was poking around in the lunch bag. "You'd like that, wouldn't you? You'd just like to let the broad go. I thought I told you to get soup and a milkshake for her. You just cannot do as you are told, can you? A Big Mac? If she gets sick, you are going to clean it up. Give me that key to the other room. You're liable to let her snitch it from your pocket."

Veda threw the key into his food bag. "Now does that make you feel better?"

They argued throughout the time they were eating; they talked as if Nonie Lee was not there. "She said she was hungry for real food; real food is not soup and milkshake."

"Who said she has to have what she wants?" Veda did not answer, just started unwrapping her hamburger and started to eat.

Nonie Lee thought, *They plan to keep me inside this room, not let me go out to eat. No chance to get away, but the talk of next time was good to hear. At least they don't plan to kill me right away. I have to remain calm, figure a way to get away from them.* Just as she was wondering where they planned for her to sleep, Veda grabbed the key from Jim's food bag and opened the door leading to the next room, then slipped the key into her white uniform pocket. "Me and you will sleep in this other room tonight, missie." She blew a large bubble with her bubblegum. "Finish your lunch now, honey. Those french fries won't be any good cold."

Tonight, that's heartening. They intend me to be alive tonight. Nonie Lee ate with gusto. *If I get sick it will be worth it, good hamburger.*

"Come on in here now," Veda said as she led her into the adjoining room. "Sit there on the bed, I'll get you a glass of water." When she handed the glass to Nonie Lee, she put a pill in her hand. "Take this, it will help you rest."

Nonie Lee threw the pill on the floor. That brought an outburst from Veda. "There's plenty more where that one came from. Now don't do that again. Open up." She placed her thumb on one side of Nonie Lee's mouth and her forefinger on the other and squeezed. When Nonie Lee started to protest, Veda thrust another pill into her mouth. She pushed the glass of water to Nonie Lee's lips, "Now swallow; it's not poison," She held her mouth shut until she swallowed.

Filled to repletion, tired and weak, Nonie Lee rested, too weary to argue or even to worry. Sleep came quickly.

Later she awoke with a start. *How long have I been asleep?* she wondered. *It's dark outside.* Loud voices were heard from the next room. She crept across the room, put her ear to the door and listened.

"Keep it down, Veda," Jim said.

"You don't need to worry; that pill will keep her asleep through the night."

"Oh yeah, it better. He will be here tomorrow and we can leave her to him."

Him who? Nonie Lee wished she knew. Could they have kidnapped her just to get her to a remote place so a hired hit man could kill her, or maybe Dan had her brought here to keep her safe? No, he wouldn't have chosen these people. *I'll wait a while before letting them know I am awake, then I'll ask.*

As it turned out she didn't have to ask. As she stood listening with her ear to the door, she heard Veda say, "Now remember you promised that if I helped you there would be no rough stuff. How do I know how she will be treated once we are gone?"

"Don't play the dumb broad. You knew this wouldn't be no picnic we're on here, you knew something unpleasant might happen, in fact would happen. And you don't know how she'll be treated once he picks her up. We'll be long gone to Mexico before he has a chance to do anything, you'll never have to know. And I would remind you that two hundred thou will buy a whole lot of enchiladas. We can go to Acapulco where you are always pestering me to take you, and you can play in the Pacific Ocean. Then a trip to Europe would be nice. That ought to make you happy for a change."

"My mistake was in believing you; I should have known better. You lie when you know the truth would be better."

"Who cares, with two hundred grand I may never want to come back," he boasted.

Answering him Veda said, "Save it for the Marines, Bubba. Funny, you are willing to take me there now, knowing we may never be able to come home again. That two hundred thousand dollars won't last forever, not the way you gamble. We'll be stuck in some foreign country with no money, no way to get home. We couldn't go home if we had the money. Oh Lord in heaven, I wish I had listened to my mamma. She warned me about you."

"Nonie Lee could hear Veda popping her gum.

Jim hollered, "I don't want to hear any more about your crazy mamma."

Nonie Lee had heard enough. She knew for sure now that it wasn't Daniel they were talking about coming for her. That could mean only bad news. Who? FBI? CIA? A hired gun? "Go check on the chick," Nonie Lee heard Jim say. She rushed back to her bed, climbed in, pulled up the covers and closed her eyes. She felt Veda take hold of her shoulder and shake her; she turned over, hiding her face in the pillow, she made a snoring sound. Apparently it worked. Now if I could just find a way out of this room later without waking them.

As soon as she thought they were asleep, she pushed a chair up to the shoulder-high window; it was too high for her to climb out. She turned a metal wastebasket upside down and placed it on a chair, climbed up and stood on it. She found the crank was missing, the one that was supposed to turn the window out. *They thought of everything. I'll just have to break it.* She carefully got off the wastebasket, stepped on the chair and then to the floor. She went into the bathroom to find something to use for a hammer to break the glass. There she found a curling iron, compliments of the motel for their guests to use. Quietly walking back to the window, she put one foot on the chair, forced her weight up with her other foot. Just as she stepped on the wastebasket it flipped out from under her foot causing her to fall on the floor with a bang.

Suddenly the bedroom door opened and an angry Jim confronted her, "What the hell do you think you're doing? Oh I see, you planned an escape through that window. Not as easy as you thought, huh? Get back in that bed. If you try that again I'll come in here and push your face in. Then we'll see how much Mr. Bookman will want you." With that he turned and walked out slamming the door, screaming obscenities. "Veda, get in there where you belong. You better quit falling asleep in that chair, you have a job to do. Remember?"

"Some job," Veda grumbled as she climbed in the twin bed next to the window.

Dejected, Nonie Lee went back to bed. No escaping tonight.

Nobody came for Nonie Lee the next day, or the next, or the next. Jim and Veda were looking more frightened and haggard every day. They kept her in the room and watched her closely; she had no way to escape. Jim always made Veda go for the food. She ate hamburgers and french fries until she could hardly stand to look at them. Veda did bring a couple of books and some magazines for her to look at, but they did something to the television in her room to keep it from working, and when they turned on the one in Jim's room they turned it low and closed the door. She couldn't hear the news; she wanted to find out if anyone was looking for her. She used her lipstick to write a note on a piece of the note pad she took from the bedside table drawer. HELP printed in bold letters. *When I get a chance I'll drop this out the window, but how will I ever be able to open it without the crank?*

On the fourth day at 3 o'clock that morning, Nonie Lee thought if she was to escape it would have to be now. She crept to the door, opened it a crack and saw that Jim was asleep in the bed and Veda was sitting in a recliner, head back, mouth open, snoring very loud. The television was still on but there was no picture, just the colored horizontal lines across the screen. *Thought she was going to sleep in here in the other twin bed. She must have fallen asleep watching television again.* She slipped into the jeans and sweatshirt that Veda gave her to wear that day, slipped on the sneakers and tied them. Then she went to her robe, felt in the pocket, and took out the nail file Veda had loaned her that morning. She walked softly to the window, climbed upon a chair and quietly started prying the catch loose. *This time I won't try to climb up on the wastebasket.* She pushed the bottom of the window out; it hung from top hinges. It made a scraping sound as the metal arms scraped against the side frame. Using her arms to heave herself up, she cautiously put one leg out when she felt strong hands clamped on the sides of her waist. Quickly, before Jim could see it, she dropped the crumpled piece of paper on which she had written the note onto the street below. Jim pulled her back into the room and struck her across the face. "I warned you; now try to pull something like that again and you'll get worse, a lot worse. Do you hear me?"

Just as he started to slap her again Veda entered and grabbed his hand. "Leave her alone. She is just trying to escape this place. You can't blame her for that. I'd like to get out of here myself."

"Oh, you think I should just let her climb out the window, take off, call the police and tell them the story of how we kidnapped her and are holding her here against her will? Is that what you want?"

"No, but you stopped her from climbing out; ain't that enough? You didn't have to hit her."

They went back to bed. Veda slept in the bed next to the window as usual; there was no chance to escape this night. *How much longer do I have before the man comes for me?*

The next morning the arguing in the other room grew louder and angrier than it had been before; Veda was calling Jim a dumb ass; telling him that the man was not coming for Nonie Lee. "We are stuck with that girl. He just wanted her out of that hospital, knowing that if we took her we would be afraid to let her go. We'll be arrested for kidnapping. You and your get-rich-quick scheme; look where it got us."

"I'm tired of your bellyaching," he shouted. "So what do you suggest? You're giving me a headache. Be quiet for a little while and let me think." She heard a scream, there was a crashing sound; it sounded like Veda fell or was knocked down.

All was quiet for a while, then she heard Veda ask in a nervous, subdued voice, "Have you come up with a plan yet?"

"Yes, we'll tie her up, gag her, pay the rent for a month and leave here. We'll head off to Mexico as planned, but without the two hundred thousand dollars. We can live cheap down there. The best place to cross the border is Eagle Pass."

"No," Veda shouted at him. "She would starve here. I will not leave here without her."

"Then you'll just have to stay here with her or we'll have to take her with us. I'm getting out of here now."

Chapter 13

Back in El Paso things were really heating up between Daniel and Lieutenant Mackey. Daniel blustered into Lieutenant Mackey's office. "Where in holy hell is Nonie Lee? I'm going crazy waiting to hear something. They've got her, haven't they?"

"Slow down, buddy. You are not to cause a big fuss." Putting his hand out to stop Daniel from coming any nearer to him he said, "The chief decided to take over; he thinks you and I are a little too chummy. He says I've been letting you call the shots concerning this case too long. His exact words were, 'Too many times you've let that store owner talk you into keeping vital information off the record.' He also said any more of that and I'd be in danger of a reprimand and possible demotion, maybe even being fired d for dereliction of duty. He's a good man and he is taking her disappearance very seriously. You can be sure he will not leave a stone unturned to find her."

"I apologize; I know everybody is doing their best. Do you have any idea where she is? I just want to know if she is safe."

"We'd all like to know if she is safe, including some fellow by the name of Rob."

"Rob who?"

"Damned if I know. All I know is the chief took a call this morning from Washington D.C., someone by the name of Rob, asking if there has been any report of a woman being involved in any kind of accident. When the chief started questioning him about why he was asking, he hung up. The chief said he got the impression that the guy was being guarded in what he said. He feels sure it has to do with this woman. To answer your question, at this point I can't tell you she is safe. I told you that if you kept meddling they would not tell me anything they don't want you to know."

Daniel remembered the mention of Rob in Nonie Lee's diary. "That's very strange. Why did the chief start questioning this Rob guy before he found out who he was and why he was asking about a missing woman?" *So Rob called? Rob again?*

"That is why he was questioning him, trying to find out who he was and why he was asking if a woman had been reported in an accident. The chief was playing it safe. He doesn't know if the man was a friend or foe. The chief advised him to file a missing person report. He immediately hung up."

"So you don't know if she is safe, you say? Some police department we have here in El Paso, can't even see that a woman is safe in the hospital. I thought from what you said the other day that you knew something, knew that she was safe."

"I didn't say that, but I admit I may have left that impression because I thought it to be true. Now I will tell you this," the lieutenant said. "If I read between the lines correctly, the CIA found out enough from debriefing the women they had planted in Tillie's establishment to apprehend the Russians trying to leave the country. And while at it, the CIA caught the FBI man they suspect of selling secrets to the Russians. The FBI claim they think the CIA had them chasing ghosts down here in Texas to keep them out of the way while they caught the fish, the big fish, the Russian spy or spies. They say the CIA wanted the glory. The Chief is not sure that is the case. He doesn't know what to think about all the bickering. There is a lot of competition between the two services, you know."

"That's a hell of a note; infighting between government agencies; some idiots are worrying about their turf being usurped while an American citizen's life is at stake."

"I know; things are tough all over. That's just the way it is."

"By the way, Nonie Lee mentioned a Rob in her diary. Rob, short for Robert I guess, same guy I'm sure. Must be a friend. And say, what about that SOB who called, threatening me?"

"We may never know; it could have been a prankster or it could have been the FBI's way of trying to scare you off. They may or may not be truly trying to get rid of Miss Talbert. They may be trying to help her; either way you were coming close to monkeying up the works. Daniel, I thought you had learned your lesson. I have to tell you that if you insist on meddling around and get your tail in a crack again, I'll throw the book at you; I'll charge you with interfering with an investigation. Got it?"

Daniel sighed, "Got it. I know you just said you don't know, but what is your best thinking? Do you think the FBI is on the up and up; are they trying to get Nonie Lee out of the way or are they trying to save her?"

Lieutenant Mackey breathed deeply and exhaled with an explosion of air. "I just told you, that's what we don't know at this point but rest assured that now that the chief is concerned about it, every thing possible will be done to keep her safe. That is why I think she has been put into hiding."

"You think, you think! I'm interested in what you know for a fact."

"Get out of here, Daniel."

Without another word, Daniel, his shoulders slumping, turned and walked down the hall and out into the hot desert sun, swearing under his breath, "Damn, they screwed up again." He got in his car and drove slowly away.

Cynthia knew something was wrong the minute she saw his face. "What's wrong, Dan?"

"Every damn thing is wrong. I should have told you before, Nonie Lee is not in her room and I can't find out where she is. We'll talk later, sis. You go on home. I'll take over now."

"I'm not leaving you here alone, Dan. You need to go in and wash your face and pull yourself together. Stay in the office and I'll tend to customers. You are in no condition to mix with the public. I'll call Albert to take the children to The Oasis for hamburgers."

After three more days of sleepless nights and frustrating days, waiting and wondering, Daniel rushed out of the store leaving Cynthia in charge, thinking, *I can't take this anymore. I have to find out if there is any word on what happened to Nonie Lee.* He roared out of the parking lot behind the store, pulled onto Mesa Street. *Damn, I better slow down; getting a ticket for speeding won't help.* Entering Lieutenant Mackey's office he was angered to see him sitting again, with his feet propped up on his desk reading a newspaper. "What the hell is going on, Mackey? Is that all you have to do, just sit there reading the paper?"

"Not again, Dan. I know you are worried, but I'm going to level with you. I don't know what is going on."

"They've lost her; I know they've lost her, you said..."

"Dan," the lieutenant interrupted, "You sound like a broken record. That was then, this is now. Things have changed, but I still think we'll find her safe and sound."

"You said the guy who called you and said he had the diary was an FBI agent."

"I said I was almost certain he was FBI; he sounded legitimate. I still think so, but I have to level with you again, I don't know if that is good or bad."

"Well, I'm asking again, who the hell does know?"

"Come on, Dan. Don't go ballistic on me. I've told you all I can. I warned you not to get too involved in this thing. I'll let you know as soon as I know something."

"I'll be waiting." He left without a goodbye, walked to his car and drove back to the store.

Chapter 14

The next morning after the discussion about taking her to Mexico with them, Jim and Vera stuffed Nonie Lee in the back seat of the car and headed east. As they drove through the Davis Mountains in the early morning, Nonie Lee, worried though she was, remarked to Veda about the many beautiful wildflowers, flowers she had not seen before. Veda told her the name of several of them; they saw pink evening primrose, yellow huisache daisy, basket flowers with their pink and yellow hues, and of course many varieties of cacti, including the yucca with its pointed leaves and panicles of white.

Veda lamented, "I am sorry that the season has passed for the Texas bluebonnets and Indian paintbrush. They are beautiful, especially when growing together in large fields."

Jim bellowed, "Here we are, running for our lives and you are whining about some damn flowers. Don't you have anything more important to think about, like trying to figure out how we are going to get across the border with this broad without being arrested? Most likely the border patrol at every border crossing has been alerted to watch for us."

"I'm sure they are watching for us. Let's turn back."

Jim growled, "Shut up."

Nonie Lee was scared but still she felt sorry for Veda. She could see that she was basically a good-hearted person who had fallen in with the wrong man.

They pulled into a rest stop at the edge of a small town; the sign read "Marathon Population 440." Nonie Lee was fascinated; she had never seen anything like it. It looked like an on-location stage setup for a western movie.

Looking out the window she saw different kinds of cacti; some had a yellow flower growing on the tip of a flat, green, oval shaped fleshy leaf. Others were tall with slender green spikes and were adorned with beautiful pink or dark rose colored blooms. *Beautiful. How I wish I could come here someday, someday? Oh someday with...* Just as she was starting to go into a dreamlike state, Jim barked, "Wake up back there. If you need to use the facilities here, get a move on."

Veda became solicitous of Nonie Lee's feelings. "Come on, dearie, let's stretch our legs." While they walked a few paces away from Jim Veda said, "Don't worry, honey, I won't let anybody harm you. If they do, it will be over my dead body."

"Thank you, Veda. That would be reassuring if I thought you had any control over what happens now, but it seems to me that Jim is calling the shots."

After a few minutes, Jim called out, "Get back here; we don't have all day." Again Veda climbed in the back seat beside Nonie Lee. *There goes my chance of jumping out of the car.*

They headed south. Veda announced, "Soon we'll be through this little town. I'm hungry. Can we stop here for lunch?"

Jim scowled, "All you think about is eating. You'll go in some place and get some sandwiches. I'll stay in the car with the broad; I'm not taking any chances on you going mush on me and letting her escape. No, you know better than to do that. You know what would happen to you if you did a stupid thing like that. I'll go."

Nonie Lee was watching for landmarks: names of towns, numbers of highways, trying to figure out where she was at all times. *If I get a chance to escape, I want to know where I am.*

After he was gone a few minutes Veda turned to Nonie Lee with a knowing look in her eye. "I'll go in an tell Jim we want a strawberry milkshake this time; I'll tell him we are tired of vanilla." She handed Nonie Lee a $20 bill saying, "Hold this for me." With that she stepped out of the car and headed for the door of the café.

Nonie Lee knew Veda was giving her a chance to get away. Her hand flew to the door handle and she hit the ground running. She was making good time, running with a speed she didn't know she possessed. The hot Texas wind was blowing sand in her face, but she wasn't concerned. *I'm free. I'm free.* She saw a gas station down the road, and made a run for it. Her toe hung up on a jagged rock, down she went, face flat on the rocky, sandy ground. She quickly jumped up and started to run when a hand closed around her mouth. "Not so fast, sister." He held her arm behind her back, yanking it so far back it felt like her rotator cuff was being separated from its mooring.

Jim huffed, "I was watching. I was testing Veda. I figured she would try to pull something like that; now I know I can't trust her. She should know by now that she can't put anything over on me." He marched her back to the car, slapped her face and pushed her in the back seat beside Veda. "Now you see what you made me do, Veda."

Veda was crying, her lip already starting to swell. Veda sobbed as she said to Nonie Lee, "I'm sorry, honey. I wanted you to get away from us. I don't know what will happen once we get to Mexico, but if this bully hurts you, he'll have to hurt me, too."

"Shut up," Jim shouted. "You won't try that again, Veda. You know if you do, the next time will be worse, maybe fatal, for both of you."

Once again, Veda tried to let Nonie Lee go. They stopped in Langtry to fill up with gasoline. While Jim was in the restroom, Veda told her, "Slap me, slap me real hard, hard enough to leave a mark on my face."

"I can't do that, Veda. You've been good to me; you've tried to let me go."

"Hurry, Nonie Lee. Do as I say. If he comes out and you are gone and he knows I let you go, he'll slap me around again, and that's the least he will do." She grabbed Nonie Lee by the shoulders and shook her. "Is that what you want, me to get beat up again? Slap me dammit, or better yet, double up your fist and hit me in the face. Then make a run for it; take your chances with a truck driver."

"All right, I'll do it." With that she hit Veda as hard as she could just below her right eye and to the side of her nose. Blood started gushing from Veda's nose. "Oh God, I'm sorry, Veda." With that she jumped out of the car and started running. She didn't stop until she got to the highway two blocks away. Hot wind blew sand in her face; she hardly noticed. She put her thumb out and made a back and forth motion with her hand, the way she had seen hitchhikers do in the movies. One car passed, then another. She was looking back at the service station, expecting any minute to see Jim run out to catch her. Thinking no one would stop for her she was about ready to turn and run back to the car when an eighteen-wheeler slowed down and the driver reached across and opened the passenger side door and said, "Where you goin' little lady?"

She jumped in the truck. "Please go; I must get away from him."

"Who you running from in such a hurry?"

She was greatly relieved when he started the truck moving. She had to think quickly. She couldn't tell him the real truth. He wouldn't believe it if she did. "My husband; I must get away before he knows I am gone."

"Why are you afraid of him? Is he a mean man?"

Nonie Lee finally turned the right side of her face toward him so he could see the bruise left from Jim's hand. Looking at his bearded face and rotund body, she thought he looked like a man who could be trusted, but best wait and see how things go, she thought. "He is very abusive," she said. She hoped he didn't ask any more questions. She wasn't sure she could keep making up lies to tell him.

"That's a nasty bruise you have there. Well I tell you, I have no use for a man who would mistreat a woman or a child. I think I would kill a man who would lay a hand on my daughter. You just relax now; you're safe as long as you are with me. If he comes around while you are with me, we'll see how brave he is in dealing with a man. Where do you want to go? I'm going all the way to Ft. Worth, that's where I live. You can go as far in that direction with me as you like. You got any money, miss?"

She felt in her pocket for the $20 bill Veda gave her. "A little."

"We'll stop when we get to Del Rio. If you are hungry, we can catch a doughnut and coffee there. As soon as I get this load unloaded, we'll head north. While you are with me, you keep your money; let me buy your food; you'll need your money later."

"You are very kind."

"Well, if my daughter was in trouble I sure would like to know that someone was willing to help her out."

"I can't thank you enough Mr. Mr...."

"The name is Jackson, Ben Jackson. Call me Ben. Would you like to tell me your name?"

"Ruthie," she lied, just in case there was something in the papers about her being missing.

They didn't talk much. He had his CB radio on most of the time. *Thank goodness he is not asking me a lot of questions.*

As they drove north she kept watching town signs, reading the population numbers. They passed through the small town of Sonora, then Eldorado. Nonie Lee saw a sign, "68 miles to San Angelo." *San Angelo, population 84,462— that looks like a good place for me to hide out for a few days.*

Ben kept looking out at his side mirror. "There is a car back there that has been showing up in my rearview mirror for the past thirty minutes or so. Could be just coincidence but let's don't take any chances. We'll give them the slip just in case that louse of a husband of yours is having you followed."

Ben pulled up beside a truck with a big red rig. "Do you trust me to put you in the hands of someone I know you can trust?"

Nonie Lee felt she had no choice, that car behind them did look like Jim's car; she couldn't be sure. "I have no reason not to trust your judgment."

'They're getting closer; put your head down so they can't see you. I have a plan. That's ol' Clem in that truck there in front of us. I'll ask him to give you a ride on into San Angelo." With that he picked up his CB and started to talk. "Crazy Man, Crazy Man, come in. This is Tex Big Boy. I have a favor to ask of you. I have a little lady here in my cab; she's running from her mean devil husband. Could you give her a ride to San Angelo? We are trying to ditch a car that seems to be following us."

"Shore's shootin', man. I owe you one for getting that maniac off my tail a couple of weeks ago."

"Thanks, buddy. If we lose that car I'll pick her up again there. Let's say we stop at Lillian's Café. Looks like they are stopping behind a short way behind us. There're two people in that car; if it is her husband, he must have picked up a girlfriend on the way." Nonie Lee had her head down and didn't dare look up to see who was in the car.

"Keep your head down and wait for me to get out of the truck. I'll go around behind and open the back door to the trailer and start looking inside; that should distract them long enough for you to slip around the front of Clem's truck and crawl in on the other side. I'll go inside and get my thermos filled. That'll give them time to come up here and look in my truck and see that no one is here."

Back on his CB Ben said, "All right then, Clem, I tell you what I'm gonna do, I'm gonna ask you to open your door on the passenger side. The little lady will step out and scurry around and slip into your truck. See you at Lillian's."

At Lillian's in San Angelo the three of them finished a lunch of chicken fried steak, mashed potatoes and gravy, pie and iced tea. Ben gave a hearty laugh, "We lost the creep back there in Del Rio. I wish I could have seen that guy's face when he saw that he had been chasing a decoy. I bet he thought he had just imagined he had seen a woman in my truck."

Nonie Lee asked, "What do you think of this as a place for me to hide out for a few days, Ben?"

"Looks good to me; chances are that rat husband of yours will not come here looking for you as he has already covered this route and didn't find you."

" I do appreciate so very much what you have done for me; what both of you have done for me." She turned to Ben. "I want you to know my real name is not Ruthie. I feel terrible about lying to you but thought it best at the time. You'll understand why later. If you will give me your address I'll write you when it is safe for me to do so, and you can tell Clem what the story is."

"All right, little lady, I'll wait to hear from you. If you think this is the place you want to stay, I'm sure Miss Lillian here will give you a job if you want one." He scribbled his address on a napkin and handed it to her. He motioned for the woman at the cash register to come over. She sat down in the booth beside Nonie Lee, "What's up, Ben?"

"I wanted to do you the favor of recommending this little lady for a job with you. She needs to get away from a rat, her husband, hide out so to speak." He winked at Nonie Lee and gave her a knowing look. "What do you think, Miss Lillian?"

"Your recommendation is good enough for me, Ben." Looking at Nonie Lee she asked, "What is your name, honey?"

"Ruthie," she lied again.

"Well, Ruthie, we don't want any trouble with an irate husband, but I could sure use some more help around here. Have you ever waited tables?"

"I worked in a restaurant, waiting tables, while in school. It's been awhile but I think I can still remember how it's done."

"Atta girl," Ben looked at her with pride and patted her shoulder.

I wish I could tell this nice man the truth now, but the time will come, if all goes well.

Lillian said, "Well, I think it's like riding a bicycle, once you know how, it's easy to pick up the knack again."

Nonie Lee had a few minor mishaps while getting the hang of it again, like the time she stacked four dirty plates on her left arm and headed for the kitchen. She forgot one should stack any glasses containing liquid on the one nearest her shoulder; she set them on the plate nearest her hand and one of them toppled over spilling water in front of her. When she took her next step, she stepped in the water, slipped and down she went, broken dishes scattered everywhere. As she struggled to get to her feet, a roar of laughter and applause rose from the diners. Besides being embarrassed, her first thought was that Lillian would surely fire her. She looked up to see Lillian smiling. Now what? Make the best of it. She turned to face the crowd, slapped her forehead with the palm of her left hand, smiled and placing her right hand across her waist, bowed low, waved as she straightened up, and said loudly, "Thank you, thank you, thank you."

Another round of applause. "More, more," they chanted.

"Sorry folks, no encore." She waved as she made her way to the kitchen.

Lillian followed her. "Good show, good show."

"I'm so sorry, Lillian; I should have known better than stack the dishes like that."

"Not to worry. It gave my customers something to laugh about; we need a little hilarity like that every once in a while."

"Thank you for taking it that way; I won't let it happen again."

"I hope not for your sake. Might break more than dishes next time," she chuckled.

Everything went along well for a few days after that. She waited tables and learned to enjoy the camaraderie of the customers and other helpers. *I must call and let Daniel know where I am and that I am all right*, she thought. *Just in case his phone line is tapped I'll say something only he will understand. Something like, "Come September, all is well."* During a lull in business she went to a pay phone hanging on the wall near the front door. Just as she dropped a quarter in the slot and started to dial the operator to ask for the number of The Bookmark Book Store in El Paso, she felt a hand clamp over her mouth, a rough hand on her shoulder and a knee in her back. Soon she was out the door and being shoved toward Jim's car. She turned in time to see Lillian looking out the front window shaking her head as Jim pushed her into the back seat and slammed the door. *Lillian thinks this is just an irate husband and doesn't want to interfere in a family brawl. That's good; it wouldn't do for her to start making a noise. It would blow my cover, for what it's worth at this point. If I get out of this I'll explain to her why I had to lie about my name.*

Chapter 15

Daniel took care of the closing time preparations and was ready to walk out the door when he got an overwhelming desire to talk to someone about Nonie Lee. He knew it was after regular office hours, but he couldn't contain himself any longer, he needed reassurance, which he was not getting from the lieutenant. He wanted to know what Dr. Tilford thought Nonie Lee might be going through, if she was still alive, and how the doctor thought an ordeal like she might be suffering would impact her recovery. He switched the sign on the door to Closed and walked back to his desk. There he dialed Dr. Tilford's number.

"Doctor Tilford here."

"Doc, it's Dan. Sorry to call so late."

"Dan, what the heck? Are you still at the store?"

"Yes, I had some last minute things to do here. I'm wondering what you think the chances of Nonie Lee still being alive are?"

"Dan, don't go borrowing trouble. Let's just wait and see what tomorrow brings. I know you are worried and frustrated, but our hands are tied at this time. Go home, sit down and have a good stiff drink. Then take a long warm bath; that will relax you so maybe you can get a good night's sleep. If you need something to help, I can call a prescription to a drug store and have it delivered."

"No thanks, I'll try your suggestion; a warm bath sounds good. But one thing I would like your opinion on before I go home. If Nonie Lee is in the wrong hands, and if we ever get her back alive, what effect do you think the trauma she must be going through will have on her recovery?"

"Dan, listen up. As I said, don't borrow trouble. Sit tight until we hear something one way or another. Of course any trauma is not good for her at this point in her recovery, but she strikes me as being a strong woman and now that she is alert I think she'll be able to survive most anything they can throw at her."

The next few days Daniel worked at a frenzied pace getting everything in order for the holidays. With Christmas only two months away there was a lot to do in the store, being sure he had enough of the latest best sellers on hand, as well as sufficient gift bags, cards, and ribbon. Extra tables were brought in for the displays of special Christmas books, one for adults and two for children. He found it helpful to keep busy. Thank Heavens, he thought, Cynthia will come in an extra day to decorate the windows and inside the store.

He checked with Lieutenant Mackey every day to see if he had any word on who may have kidnapped Nonie Lee, but he was careful to keep calm when talking to him. Then after almost a week passed and still no word about her, Daniel walked into the lieutenant's office. "Don't call in the Mod Squad; I'm not going to create a scene this time. I have just about given up." He understood how his constant badgering was getting on Lieutenant Mackey's nerves.

"That's welcome news. Hey, I'm glad to see you. I just called the store. I wanted to give you the good news. Miss Talbert is with the Texas Rangers, safe and sound, being debriefed about what she experienced and what she heard while in the company of the kidnappers."

"Thank God. That's the best news I could hear. When can I see her?"

"Don't get all eager; I don't know, but it will probably be a day or two, maybe more."

"Kidnappers? So she had been kidnapped? And what do the Texas Rangers have to do with it?"

"The chief feared that with all the infighting going on between the CIA and the FBI, they would let the perpetrator get away, he thought maybe intentionally, to protect their backside, if it turned out to be one of their own. That's why the chief brought in the Texas Rangers; they got right on the case. They were keeping a watch on her for about a week before she disappeared from the hospital. They followed the kidnappers from the hospital to a motel in Sierra Rojo on Route 10, this side of El Paso. There they caught the culprit who hired the two-bit crooks. He is one Lew Frazer, known to be a gun for hire. He has been on the FBI's most wanted list for some time. The Rangers took him into custody before he could get to Miss Talbert."

"What about the other two scumbags?"

"Same thing. All three will be guests of Uncle Sam for some time to come. The Rangers just had to keep an eye on the kidnappers to see what they would do when they realized that they would not be relieved of their charge, like they had been promised. They wanted to see if they contacted a bigger fish after Frazer didn't show up, but evidently they didn't know who the bigger fish was."

"Halleluiah and amen. Now we are getting somewhere. When can I see her?"

COME SEPTEMBER

"Hold on, you've already asked that. Don't you want to know what has been going on?"

"Sure do."

"Sit down, here have a cup of coffee. This is a long, but interesting story."

"As I told you before, the chief got tired of the two factions, FBI and CIA, muddying up the water with their bickering; he was almost as tired of them as he was of you sticking your nose in," he said with a chuckle. "So he brought in the Rangers."

"The Rangers watched a couple of local characters that they knew were skulking around the hospital asking questions of the maids and janitors. They purposely had the guard announce to one and all of the helpers that he would be late the next morning, said he had some personal business to take care of. Sure enough, the crumb-bums took the bait. The man pretending to be the guard kidnapped Miss Talbert. He had a helper, one Miss Veda Johnson. The Texas Rangers watched them all the way, while they were in Sierra Rojo until they tried to cross the border with her. They knew those two were just hired thugs; they wanted to catch the person for whom they were working.

"When days passed and the big fish didn't show to relieve the kidnappers of their charge, the two of them became even more concerned. They thought he got scared or maybe he didn't intend to come for her to begin with; maybe he intended all along to leave them holding the bag, knowing they would have to get rid of her in some way, otherwise they would be caught and charged with kidnapping. The Rangers wanted to be sure, so they waited to see what would happen, all the time keeping an eye on Miss Talbert to see that she was not harmed."

"How could they be sure of that?"

"By posing as an electrician, a Ranger placed a listening device in the rooms occupied by the three. They put an operative in the rooms on both sides of those two rooms. That way they kept tabs on what they planned to do. So you see, Miss Talbert was never in any real danger. I was sure the chief was on top of the situation."

"And what made you so sure? I sure as hell wasn't sure anybody was doing anything."

"The chief's demeanor was one of calm and confidence when we discussed it."

"Sounds like they very near let them get out of the country before stopping them."

"Not the case. They alerted the border patrol to watch for them in case they

97

got away from the Rangers, which was not likely to happen."

"I know, I know the Texas Rangers always get their man."

"Right."

"The Rangers must be better at tailing their prey than the yahoo was at stalking me."

"I'm sure. By the way, it might interest you to know that the doc has examined Miss Morgan, ah, rather Miss Talbert, and has given her a clean bill of health. Says she will not have to return to the hospital when she is free; she'll be free to go home."

"Oh wow! That is good news. I hope she doesn't take off as soon as she is released. The doc? Did he know about this all along?"

"Not on your life, fellow. The Rangers demanded that no one but them and the chief know about the operation. They had Dr. Tilford brought on board when they picked Miss Talbert up at the border. They wanted him to examine her to be sure she is all right. Now that brings you up to date. I wanted to let you know so you can relax."

"Thanks, I appreciate that." Daniel was thrilled. *Hot dog, it's a beautiful day, rain and all.* He could hardly contain himself. One thing lingered in his mind, however. He groused, "What about this Rob guy? Who is he?"

"That is something we'll have to find out later. Possibly a relative or a boyfriend." He thought it best to prepare Daniel for that possibility. "Maybe even her husband."

"Damn, I hope he is a relative, not boyfriend, and I sure as hell hope he is not her husband."

"Yeah, I thought you might be interested in that, but just hang loose. We'll know soon enough."

Finally the day came when Lieutenant Mackey walked into the store. Daniel was getting ready to open the door for business. "Hey fellow, I thought you'd like to know they got a confession out of the man who hired the two kidnappers."

"Who is he? Anyone I would have heard of?"

"No, he is just a go-between, name of Lew Frazer, wanted for extortion and murder. Claims not to know who hired him; he is probably telling the truth about that. That's the way those paragons of virtue operate. If they want some dirty work done, they hire somebody, who hires somebody, who hires somebody. Makes it very hard to get to the top dog. 'Just a voice on the phone,' this Frazer lowlife claims. We may never know who it is, but I can guess that the authorities will get their man one way or the other. We may hear of a senator or a cabinet member or some other Washington biggie suddenly deciding to resign, no doubt due to health reasons or to spend more time with family," he chuckled.

Daniel said, "That does have a familiar ring to it. But tell me, how does this Frazer guy get paid?'

"There are different ways; the most commonly used one I think, is having a stoolie meet the recipient of the loot and hand over the cash. The stoolie better damn sure deliver the goods or he may wake up with a horse head on his pillow, so to speak."

"Is that all you came in to tell me? I was hoping for some even better news about Nonie Lee."

"Oh man, what do you expect of me, that I should pull Miss Talbert out of a hat like a magician pulls out a rabbit?" "Something like that."

" I've heard from the chief that they will try to get that woman, Veda, to turn state's evidence on that Jim guy. I understand that she treated Miss Talbert well, as well as she could under the circumstances, even tried to help her escape that monster, Jim Parker. They say Miss Talbert will ask for leniency for her."

"The store is looking good, looking a lot like Christmas. I can almost hear those jingle bells and smell the plum pudding."

"That's because "Jingle Bells" is being piped in on the sound system, and I just mixed apple cider and spices and put it on to heat. Later on today we'll serve plum pudding and wassail to the customers. Want to get them in a Christmas mood. You can cut the small talk, Mackey. I know you are not here to enjoy the sounds and smells of Christmas. You can tell me about it while you have a cup of wassail."

"You're right. I'm wondering if you have that last bestseller by Richard Evans, something to do with Christmas. I thought I'd pick up a couple of copies, one for my wife and one for Miss Talbert."

"One for Nonie Lee? You've seen her, you son-of-a-gun! I didn't think you came in just to buy books, either. Let's have it. What do you know about Nonie Lee?"

"There's good news and bad news."

"Let me have it."

"Do you promise to behave yourself if I do?"

"Come on, man, don't mess with me. Spit it out."

"As I said, there's good news and bad news. Miss Talbert is safe with two female Texas Rangers. They have been keeping her company ever since the rescue. You know Dan, it's looking more and more like you were on the right track when you said someone was looking to have Miss Talbert done away with. What made you think the FBI or some politician would consider having someone killed because that person has dirt on them?"

Daniel rubbed his chin. "It's thought to have happened before. I remember my dad telling me about a madam who was to testify about something, I don't know what, back in the fifties, I think. Dad knew only what he read in the papers. The day before she was to testify before a Senate subcommittee she was a passenger in a small plane that went down just outside Alexandria, Virginia. There was suspicion that some politician or politicians, or some other biggie in Washington had her murdered, but there was no hard evidence. Actually there was no investigation. One wonders why."

"I see. We know some politicians can get rough when their position is endangered; they can't stand to give up that power and the gravy train after retirement. Did you read Martha Mitchell's autobiography? In it she declared that she was kept doped up in a hotel room in a California for four days to keep her from spilling the beans about Watergate. Yep, some of them can play rough when their turf is challenged."

Daniel listened patiently to what the lieutenant said, almost afraid to hear the bad news part. "You told me the good news. Now what's the bad news you alluded to?"

The lieutenant's eyes twinkled. "I hate to tell you the bad news, but here goes, you can't see Miss Talbert until tonight. The Ranger ladies are seeing that she gets where she needs to go to shop and to get her hair put back to its natural color. You may not know her when you see her," he teased. "She said she doesn't want to see you while looking like she did the day you picked her up in front of The Bookmark, or in the picture on the dust jacket of her book, *Come September.*"

Daniel was delighted that the bad news he expected was really the best news he had heard since this whole thing started. "Shopping, for cripes sake? And the beauty parlor?"

Lieutenant Mackey laughed. "Not to worry. She's as eager to see you as you are to see her. Remember she had no luggage with her; she does need a few things, you know. She expected to catch the red-eye back to Seattle that night after going to all the bookstores in El Paso to promote her book. She planned to just drop in, introduce herself and say hello, and leave a copy of her book. No book signings scheduled. She planned to use Seattle as a base of operation and make one-day visits to other cities in the coming days. She was staying close to the island, thinking she could seek sanctuary there if the need arose. By the way, how are sales going with the book?"

"Fine, fine; tell you the truth I've hardly noticed. I've been too absorbed in Nonie Lee's whereabouts and well-being to worry about book sales. Say, ever find out who that Rob fellow is?"

"I wondered how long it would take you to start wondering about that. They think he may be her boyfriend. What do you make of that?" The lieutenant looked like the cat that couldn't quite swallow the canary.

"If that is true then I'll just have to work that much harder to win my lady's affections. I see that smirk; you're pulling my leg, aren't you?"

"Could be. I have to tell you, though I hate to...." He watched for the reaction on Daniel's face. "He's her brother."

"You son-of-a-biscuit eater, and you call yourself a friend. I'm so happy to hear the news; tell you what—I'll forgive you. You say I can see her tonight?"

'That's what I said, buddy." He was pleased to see the happy look on Daniel's face.

"Great. Where can I see her?"

"She'll be staying at the Cortez."

"I talked with her earlier this morning. Want to hear what she said?"

"Does an elephant have big ears?"

"Okay, I get the message. Here goes; I made a recording. You can hear her exact words." He turned the small tape player on and the tape began to turn. Her voice came through loud and clear. *"In the car, after we left the motel, the effects of the orange colored pill did its job with lightning speed. I don't know how long I was in that drug-induced sleep, but when I awoke I felt like I was enveloped in a soupy fog. The mountains, which I later heard Jim and Veda refer to as the Davis Mountains, looked far away. I looked out the window in this hazy state of mind for what seemed to last for hours. Jim said, 'Make her take another pill; she is beginning to wake up.' Veda argued, 'We have to let her eat something first.' I was happy to hear that, I was very hungry. We pulled into a drive-in along the road. After we finished eating the hamburgers and milkshakes, Veda took another pill from her purse, held it up to my mouth, handed me a cup of water and spoke very loudly, 'Just take it, honey. It's mild, won't really knock you out; it'll just relax you.' She winked at Jim. Then she surprised me; she palmed the pill and put it in her pocket. It was late and I would have been too tired to resist if she had insisted I take the pill.*

"They talked about Eagle Pass being the best place to cross the

border, that it would be a busy bridge because a lot of tourists cross there to visit Piedras Negras. At last we drove up behind a line of cars; I later found out it was at the Mexican border. By this time I was beginning to come out of the stupor I had been in for hours. Suddenly the door was jerked open; a man in a uniform yelled at Jim, 'Get out of the car with your hands up.' Jim complied immediately.

"That's when Dr. Tilford stepped up, opened the back door and took my arm, 'It's over. You're safe now. Dan is waiting for you back in El Paso, not too patiently, I must add.' I literally shouted joy, joy, and joy. That, I do believe, was the happiest moment of my life."

Daniel was overjoyed to hear those words. "Dear, sweet Nonie Lee, I hope she will have many even happier moments in the future, with me."

"I won't even try to dissuade you, buddy. Your instincts about her were correct. I know now she is right for you and that she is as enamored of you as you are of her. Congratulations, my boy!"

"I'll call her at the Cortez later and go to see her after I close the store at 6:30. Will she be there by then? Do you think she'll be happy to see me?"

"Slow down, my friend. Yes, I think she will be there by 6:30, but you'll have to call to see. To your second question, I wouldn't be at all surprised. She could talk of nothing but seeing you when she found out she was free to leave the safe house where the Rangers have been keeping her; they wanted to be sure all the loose ends were tied up before bringing her out in the public."

"Won't she still be in danger? Isn't the high muckety-muck who hired the thug and kidnappers still out there?"

"He wouldn't dare show his lousy self now. In fact they most likely already have a bead on him. They may never be able to prove he was the instigator, but you can bet he'll be keeping a low profile from now on."

"Have you notified her folks that she is here and she is safe?"

"The FBI spoke with her attorney, Mr. Thompson. He will see that her family gets the message."

Daniel said, "Just a minute, who is that joker who has been following me around everywhere I go?"

"An FBI agent. *Adiós, amigo.*" Lieutenant Mackey waved and started to the door.

"Wait, there must be more that I need to know, like what are they going to do about Tillie's gang, the women collaborators I mean?"

The lieutenant turned around and with a broad smile said, "There are some things we'll just have to wait and hope to read in the newspapers or hear it on television."

"Yeah, in the funny paper, if they keep performing like they have been lately. As you know, the guy who followed me around made a poor tail. A five-year-old could have spotted him."

"Did you ever stop to think maybe he wanted you to see him?"

"To what purpose?"

"That we'll have to learn later, or maybe never. The FBI doesn't feel it necessary to explain their actions to local police, not even to the Texas Rangers. In fact, they would like to keep us out of it altogether, but in this case we were the finders, so to speak. A certain amount of cooperation was necessary, especially after the Rangers came into the picture."

"I see. I'd still like to know how it all went down; how the FBI explain their being with Tillie's girls in the first place? Won't their wives be a little miffed, to say the least? And to say nothing of the Justice Department; how do they explain their presence in a house of ill repute; especially considering that national security could have been, and most likely was compromised?"

"Okay, here goes, the way they explain their presence there in Tillie's place goes like this: They had FBI operatives placed in there over a year ago. When they went there, they had their choice of women. Naturally, they choose the ones they had placed there. Some of the women were professional prostitutes; the Russians let things slip, not knowing that they were fraternizing with FBI women. That is the way they had of keeping track of what was going down. The operatives kept an ear out and reported back to the FBI agents. When an agent visited one of them, it was for debriefing only."

"Oh yeah?"

The lieutenant chuckled. "All in the line of duty, my friend. All in the line of duty. That's what they tell me. To quote the famous Herodotus, 'I know not what the truth may be, I tell the tale as 'twas told to me.' Take their word for it; that's what I'm doing."

"Suits me. However, I do still wonder who killed Tillie."

"They say Tillie died of natural causes. I'm taking their word for that, too. The operation was a success. The CIA, with the help of the FBI, got their spies. Maybe you'll see something about it in the *Washington Post*, but maybe not. We'll just have to wait and see. In the meantime, Dan, please keep what I told you under your hat. Seriously, I wouldn't want you or me to have a visit from the FBI. I have a feeling those guys could get pretty rough."

"One more thing," Dan hesitated. "Are you sure that Rob guy is her brother?"

The lieutenant laughed. "I thought you'd quit worrying about that. I tell you, he is her brother."

"I know, just joshing."

Daniel assured him, "Lieutenant, you may rest easy. You have nothing to worry about me discussing what our conversation was today, about the legal stuff. I'm just happy everything turned out as it has, just happy to have Nonie Lee back safe. And, whew, I'm relieved to hear that that Rob guy is her brother."

The lieutenant cracked up laughing. "Atta boy."

Chapter 16

After getting back to the store, Daniel ordered a dozen long stemmed yellow roses sent to Nonie Lee's room at the Cortez. Inside the box was a note reading, "Yellow roses for my yellow rose; soon to be yellow rose of Texas, I hope."

After closing time, he rushed home, showered, shaved and splashed cologne behind his ears. He got into his best dark suit and white shirt, added a silver gray tie and went downstairs to say goodnight to the family. Cynthia and her family were there as well and Larry and his wife. "Sorry, Dan, the children were hungry. We started dinner without you, but your plate is in the oven," Cynthia apologized.

Daniel kissed his mother's cheek. "Mom, I forgot to call and tell you. I won't be eating here tonight. I have a date with Nonie Lee. She has been sprung from the safe house." He was rushing to get to the door.

His mother called after him. "Wait, son, what do you mean, Nonie Lee was sprung from the safe house?"

"Sorry, Mom, I didn't keep you up to date on what's been going on. After Nonie Lee was rescued from the kidnappers, the Texas Rangers kept her in a safe house for her protection. Her location was hush,-hush; they didn't even tell me where she was.

"Lieutenant Mackey did tell me she had been found and was all right. They found the low-life responsible for her mugging and her kidnapping. They have determined that she is no longer in danger. This morning she was allowed total freedom to do as she pleased. She chose to go shopping and to the beauty shop. I don't have time to give you the details right now. I'm going to pick her up at the Cortez where she is staying and take her to dinner in Juarez. She has never been to Mexico."

Larry's wife, Jeannie, spoke up. "When will we meet her?"

"Yeah," Larry chuckled, "I have a feeling we'll get to know her real well one of these days."

"I hear you, bro. Don't fret; I'll bring her home to meet Mom soon. Now don't get all excited, guys, she may turn tail and run when she meets this motley crew. I'll tell you all about it later."

"Tell us about it now, Dan," Cynthia said. Then seeing he was rushing out, not waiting for an answer she called out, "Say, Bubba, you do look mighty handsome in your black suit."

"Thanks, Cynthia. It's a special date."

A chorus of applause went up from the table. "I'm glad for her, son. Go. Enjoy your evening." He blew a kiss to his mother, flashed a big smile, turned and walked out, closing the door behind him.

Daniel did a double-take when Nonie Lee answered his knock on her hotel room door. Before him stood a beautiful woman. The straight, pulled back black hair was gone and in its place a massive mane of light brown billowed around her face. There were no more black, horned rimmed glasses; instead he got the full impact of her sparkling green eyes. She wore a long black dress; the V-neck, sleeveless top molded to her upper torso, flaring below her hips, emphasizing her neat, trim figure. "How beautiful you look, Miss Nonie Lee Talbert, author of the best selling book, *Come September*." He couldn't wait to tell her he had seen that it was on the bestseller list that afternoon.

"Trudy Rose to you, sir," she laughed. "Oh, I'm so happy to see you. I don't care if the book sells or not." She reached out to him.

He held her gently in his arms and kissed her. "Shall we get better acquainted before we get married, Trudy Rose?"

"You are taking a lot for granted, Mr. Lindsey."

"Well then, will you marry me, Miss Talbert?"

"Come September." She smiled up at him as she put her arms around his neck and pulled his head forward and gave him a long tender kiss.

"That's what I've been waiting for," he murmured as he held her close and returned her kiss.

The End